GHOST

DEMENTED SOULS
BOOK TWELVE

MELISSA STEVENS

GHOST

Melissa Stevens

This Demented Souls book, like all the Souls books, is dedicated to my dad, Wilmer 'Billy' Stephens.
When I started the series I used him as a major resource, as he'd been a police officer, machinist, gun smith, Harley rider, mechanic and so much more.
Now that he's gone, I write them in his memory.

Thanks Dad.

While I was growing up my father had two of the best friends I've ever known of. They are the ones who taught me that family is more than just who you're related to. As I was working on Maverick we lost the last of them. Now that all three are gone, I miss the others nearly as much as I miss Dad.

From here on out, the Demented Souls books are dedicated to the men who taught me all about brothers by choice.
Frank Edwards (1950-2006)
Wilmer Stephens (Dad) (1952-2017)
George Claridge (1955-2022)

CHAPTER 1

Ghost sat in the cab of the truck backed into a cut in a hill about a quarter mile from where the road into the ranch met the highway, watching. It was fucking cold, but he'd been colder and at least today he had the shelter of the truck to keep the wind off him. It was a plus that he didn't need to lay motionless for hours or days on end.

Not to mention a thermos of hot coffee and a meal packed fresh this morning. Ghost reminded himself of these benefits of his current assignment every time he had the urge to say screw it or walk away.

He'd been assigned to figure out how to get rid of the asshats who had spent the last couple months harassing the women coming and going from the ranch. Today, that meant watching the two men sitting in another pickup waiting along the highway less than a quarter mile from the turn off to the ranch house, then to alert someone else, who would pick up the tail, should they leave.

It wasn't the men leaving that worried him. It was what they'd been doing, and why they were sitting there that set Ghost's teeth on edge. For a while they had taken to sitting near the entrance to Tuck's ranch and waiting for women to leave the ranch, then followed and harassed them. Recently, they'd been keeping track of who came and went and began harassing them as they arrived or anytime that they ran across them in Gillette.

Tuck, Lurch, and the rest of the Demented Souls were fed up with these guys and their bullshit. The Souls had made a couple of moves and issued a few threats, but the idiots in the truck didn't seem to be taking the hint. It was time to get serious about making them go away.

Now Lurch had set Ghost to doing some recon. Ghost wasn't sure what the plan was. So far, a few threats were all they'd done to run the men off, and it hadn't worked. They kept coming back. It was time to get serious.

While most people in this situation might call the cops, the Souls didn't work that way. That was only partly because they had no proof the men had done anything illegal. Even following and threatening the women could be dismissed as a misunderstanding, or worse, no evidence, until someone was more seriously hurt.

But Ghost had been working on a plan.

The first step was to distract the assholes while the club had some business happening that they didn't want these ass wipes to notice. After business had wrapped up, they needed to find a way to drive these idiots back to wherever they called home. Once he figured out who they cared about and who was pulling their strings, then he'd get down to the real work.

That would be making these men, and whoever was directing them, decide that the Demented Souls weren't worth the trouble of fucking with them.

Ghost was going to enjoy it. He so rarely got to fuck with people these days. He missed it.

🐾

"I'm not sure this is the best plan. There's only a dusting of snow now, but who knows what will happen once you hit the road. We could have a storm move in and dump two feet in a couple hours. You'd be stranded away from the ranch with no back up." Lurch shook his head as he spoke. "I know you like to work solo, but there's no way you're doing this alone."

"This is the best time to do it. They're going to assume with the holiday coming up that we're going to keep everyone close. I'm confident these shit heads will take the chance to go back to wherever they call home and regroup. Maybe they'll send someone else to take over. We may not get a chance this good for a long time. If ever."

"I'm not arguing that. I agree it may be the best time. But it doesn't change my mind about you doing this alone. That's still a hard no."

Ghost started to speak again, but Lurch held one hand up, stopping him. "Think that over for a minute before you argue. I'm not saying no. I'm saying you need to take someone with you. You need to have back up if you run into trouble. Pick someone. You know who you'll work best with, so I'll leave the choice of who up to you, but you are not going alone, so there is no point in trying to talk me out of this."

Ghost fell silent. He pressed his lips together to keep the shitty comment he was thinking from slipping out. He didn't know more than a couple of the men here well. The one he knew the best was Tuck, and he couldn't pull him away from the ranch. Not when he needed to be here for so many reasons.

Then there was Lurch, who Ghost trusted, but again, he couldn't pull him away from the ranch, he didn't trust any of the rest of the men to cover his back in an emergency. Yes, they would do their best, but he hadn't fought with them. He didn't know their reaction time or what they would do should there be a situation. He didn't want to have to take one of them with him. He hated having to rely on someone he didn't know well to guard his back.

Ghost looked around the table in the bunkhouse that served as their temporary clubhouse and meeting place. His gaze lingered on each face around the table, thinking about each one in turn and trying to gauge how well he might work with each.

"Can I give it some thought and come to you later with a choice?"

"Yes," Lurch said with a nod, then turned back to the table. He continued with other club business. "We've got a load of cargo at the line shack near the south pasture. We need to get it moved out before the holiday. I'm going to need at least two of you for that. I'll get back with you on who will handle that once I know who will be working with Ghost."

Men around the table nodded, glancing at each other but no one spoke until after Lurch spoke again.

"Anything else that needs our attention?"

"I think we've hit everything we needed to tonight," Tuck said from the far end of the table.

"I do have one more bit of business I'd like to bring up," Lurch said after a moment. "It's something I'm sure we've all thought but no one has been willing to say, not out loud. We need more help. We've got enough for club business or enough to run the ranch, mostly, but not for both. Trying to cover both with too few men is wearing us out and will lead to mistakes. I don't want it to get that far. If any of you know of anyone who might be tapped for either position, come talk to me. Ideally, they would be someone we could accept as a prospect and eventually patch in, but we need bodies for the work so if we can't find prospects, we might be forced to just hire hands. I'm not sure how we'll handle club business if we've got non-club hands around, but we'll figure it out."

The new president glanced around the table, giving everyone a chance to speak up, then thumped the whiskey bottle he was using as a makeshift gavel against the table. "Meeting dismissed. I'll hang around for a bit, in case anyone wants to talk to me informally, then I'm going home to Kerry. There may not be much snow on the ground, but it's colder than fuck and I want to get warm."

A hint of a smile curved Ghost's lips. It was beyond fucking cold outside, and he didn't envy Lurch or Tuck the walks back to their homes. At least it was warm enough in here that he wouldn't have to hurry as he stripped down and slipped between the sheets, but by morning it would cool off enough that he'd hustle to get dressed and get a fire started.

Tuck made his excuses and left shortly after the meeting ended. Lurch stayed a few minutes longer, but was gone by nine p.m.

Ghost didn't like having to take someone with him while he tailed these assholes staking out the Souls and figured out where they came from, but he did see the wisdom in it. It wasn't that he didn't like the idea of taking any of the available men with him or leaving them shorthanded at the ranch, though that was part of it.

Ghost sat silent, his chair situated in a corner where he could watch the other men as they relaxed, watched TV, played a couple video games, chatted until they were ready to call it a night. No. He didn't like the idea of any of them backing him up in the field. Not unless he had no choice.

If he could choose anyone, he'd have Malice at his back. Malice had been the best spotter Ghost had ever worked with, and not just because the man could see a hair twitch on a tick's back at a thousand yards. Though that didn't hurt. Malice was the closest thing Ghost had ever had to a brother before he'd found the Demented Souls.

Ghost hadn't seen Malice in more than ten years. Not since he had left the Marines and Malice had stayed. They had been in touch, but hadn't seen each other since.

Now that he thought about it, he would swear Malice had mentioned getting discharged. Maybe he should reach out and see what his old friend was doing these days.

He pulled his phone out and typed out a message, asking his old friend what he'd been up to, and where he was. He hoped Malice would get back to him soon and would be available. When he was finished with the message and had hit send, he pocketed the phone once more and turned his attention back to the men still milling around the clubhouse. There was nothing here to hold his interest. They'd settled in playing some faux combat game that after having seen the real thing, he had no interest in.

While he hadn't done anything strenuous, he'd spent a good chunk of the day sitting in the near freezing cab of a truck. Staying warm took more energy than most people realized. He pushed himself to his feet and headed for the bathroom. A hot shower and bed were his plan for the night.

CHAPTER 2

When Ghost got up the next morning, he dressed, went into the bunkhouse kitchen, and started the coffee pot. The large pot they used took longer to brew than he cared for, but a smaller pot had to be remade too often. He turned on the tv, changed the channel to the news, and turned up the sound before picking up his phone from where he'd left it on the charger the night before and taking a seat in one of the overstuffed recliners.

He paid little attention to the reporter on the screen rambling about the winter storm ravaging the northeast and scrolled through his notifications.

Malice had texted him back.

Malice: Hey old man, it's been a while. How are you doing?

Malice: Yeah, I'm free, so to speak. Discharged a few months ago. Looking for something new. What are you up to?

Ghost replied.

Ghost: I'm working in Wyoming these days. A place with openings if you're game. It's real work, physical most days but the pay is good.

A soft beep alerted him that the coffee was ready. He stood and fixed himself a cup, knowing from experience the other men would be up soon and if he didn't hurry, he might not get a second cup. He would need at least a second cup, and hopefully a third, if he could get it. Between what they would drink and filling thermoses, they would need at least two of the commercial size pots.

Once the other men were up and moving around, the coffee would disappear fast, but he would wait until they were up to make the second pot. Until then, he would enjoy his coffee and listen to what was happening in the world.

Before anyone else got up, Ghost's phone buzzed in his pocket. When he pulled it out, he found Malice had messaged him back.

Malice: When did you get so close?

Malice: Last I heard you were somewhere close to the border.

Ghost: Close to where? Where are you?

Ghost: I've been in Wyoming a few months.

Ghost: Came up in early September.

Ghost: From where I've been in Arizona.

Malice: I'm in Billings. Been tending bar for the last couple months looking for something that pays better.

Ghost bit back a wry laugh. How ironic that the help he wanted at his back was only a few hours away and looking for a job?

Malice: What's the job?

Ghost: A ranch. Winter work for now, but steady pay and job security.

He debated with himself if he should say more. It had been ten years since he'd last seen Malice and wondered for a moment if he was still someone he could trust. Maybe it would be best to get him here and find out before Ghost told his old friend more.

Malice: You sure there's enough work for me?

Ghost: There's work, but it's cold and physical. Not like tending bar. You interested?

Malice: Possibly. Where in Wy are you?

Ghost: Open A Bar T ranch, just outside of Gillette. Come see if it's something you're interested in.

Malice: I'll do that. Got a couple things to take care of here, but I'll be there in the next day or two. Who should I talk to?

Ghost: Foreman's name is Lurch. I'll tell him you're coming.

Malice: Great. See you in the next couple days. Want to have a drink?

Ghost: Let's play it by ear. If things go well, we may be roommates again.

He shoved his phone back into his pocket as Jake shuffled in from the bedroom. The newest fully patched brother went straight to the coffee pot and poured himself a cup, then took it with him as he continued into the bathroom.

Ghost shook his head. He wouldn't have taken a drink into the bathroom, but who was he to tell another what to do? Well, at least when it wasn't a work situation. Then he didn't hesitate to issue whatever orders he saw fit.

He stood and refilled his cup, and watched as the rest of the men made their way into the front room and retrieved coffee.

Watt came in, fully dressed and after a trip to the restroom he went to the sink and filled thermoses with hot water, preparing them to fill with coffee.

Ghost left him to finish that job and went into the bunk room to get his Thinsulate. He would need it when they went out to breakfast, and probably after for whatever his assignment was today. Probably another day in the truck watching assholes looking to harass them. He was not looking forward to another day sitting in the cold. He wasn't looking forward to that.

CHAPTER 3

Robyn dragged herself out of the house and to work. It wasn't that she didn't like her work, she did most of the time, but having to drive on the snow and ice terrified her. Not because she wasn't confident of her own abilities. She knew from experience she could handle anything life threw at her. What terrified her was the people who thought they could drive in the ice but couldn't. They were a danger to themselves and everyone else on the roads.

She dealt with those people every day, but had to be polite and keep a smile on her face no matter how badly she wanted to tell them to go home and stay off the roads, even in the summer.

She shook her head at the direction her thoughts had taken. Telling these people what she thought would do no good. They would do what they wanted no matter what she, or anyone, said to them. She'd long since given up.

She parked in her usual space at the end of the building, killed the engine, and pulled her hood and scarf tighter around her face before getting out of the car and hurrying to the door.

"Hey, Harry, how has it been today?" she asked as she stepped behind the counter and realized she and the man she was replacing for the evening shift were the only ones in the little convenience store.

"Slow. Not many out with it this cold. What few are out aren't stopping if they don't have to. You know how it is."

Robyn nodded. She knew.

"Anything new since last night?" She peeled off her outer layers, taking them in the back room where they would be out of the way until she needed them again. She clocked in and went back out front.

"Nothing. I made coffee about twenty minutes ago, so it's fresh."

"Thanks, the night shift will start coming in soon."

"I've already had a couple. They said they were starting early in case of ice and traffic. Can't say I blame them."

Robyn looked out the big glass windows at the huge piles of dirty snow the plows had left sitting wherever they could.

"Me either." She would have left earlier if she'd had more than just the couple of blocks between here and her apartment to go. In the summer it was close enough she walked when she worked the day shift. When she was going to be making the trip after dark, sometimes she even walked then, but not always.

Driving in the summer was more about her mood, and other plans like errands before or after work, than the time of day, temperature or even safety. Robyn rarely worried about her safety in Dickenson.

She knew nearly everyone and had no doubt that if she needed help, she could go to nearly any door and ask for it. Hell, half the time someone stopped while she was walking and offered her a ride. Some had gotten used to her preference to walk, but others still stopped every time they saw her. While she appreciated the gesture, sometimes she wished they would just let her be.

"You have any plans for tonight?" Robyn asked as Harry started bundling up, preparing for the cold and his trip home.

"Nothing big. Madison said something about dinner and watching something. I'll probably fall asleep halfway through whatever it is." He shook his head. "I swear, I sleep more in the winter than the summer. I feel like I'm sleeping half my life away."

"We all sleep more in the winter. It's partly because of less light, partly because it takes more energy to do everything. I don't know about you or Madison, but I have a thing about hot baths in the winter. The colder it is, the more I want to soak in a tub of hot water." Robyn shrugged but couldn't help wondering if he would find her confession strange.

Harry shook his head. "I'm ready for more sunshine. I'm tired of so much dark and cold."

"I'm sure I'll get to that point before spring gets here. I always do. But for now, I'm enjoying it. It's a nice change and I like the snow. It also means we slow down a bit. Anything special I need to get done tonight?"

"Nothing out of the usual. And shouldn't be as much of that. We haven't sold much in the last few days so restocking shouldn't take long. Hope you have something to keep yourself entertained."

"No worries. I brought my e-reader and it's fully loaded."

"I'm not sure what to wish you, a busy evening so things go fast, or a quiet one so you get lots of reading in."

"I'm okay with either. You head home and enjoy your night. Tell Madison I said hi and hope she's doing well."

"Will do." Harry glanced around, making sure he hadn't left anything behind, then paused at the door before turning back to look at Robyn. "Have a good night, call if you need anything."

"Will do." She watched him go then turned back to the store in front of her. There was no one in the store so she might as well start on the list of things she needed to do tonight. The sooner she got it all done, the sooner she could get to her book.

CHAPTER 4

The sun was less than an inch from the western horizon when Ghost's phone rang. He frowned and picked it up. He wasn't expecting any calls and he wondered what was up now. The number on the screen was Lurch's. He wouldn't be ignoring that.

"Hey, boss, how's it going?"

"So far so good. That man you suggested for a job, the one you called?"

"Malice?"

"That's the one. How well do you know him?"

"I couldn't tell you what size shoes he wears or where he went to high school, but I trust him with my life. He's saved it a couple times, and I've done the same for him."

"I'm glad to hear that, but what about the rest of us? What about the women? Would you trust him with their lives?"

Ghost took a deep breath and thought about the question before saying anything more. "Yeah. I do. I wouldn't have recommended him if I didn't trust him to do everything we need done here."

"Good. I hired him. His first assignment is to go with you to track the assholes harassing London and Celia back to wherever they came from and put an end to this shit for once and for all."

"I wasn't aware he was here already. When do you want us to leave?"

"Today. Follow them wherever they go when they leave. Turnabout is fair play. Let them know how it feels to be followed and harassed. Follow them until they go back to wherever they came from, then make the point."

"Even if it takes weeks? What if something comes up here?"

"As long as it takes. If we need either of you, I'll call you back. Right now, I'm more concerned with getting rid of them. Secondary is finding out where they came from and who sent them. There are other goals, but they're farther down the list."

"Ten four. Is Malice ready to leave town already? Did you ask?"

"I did. He said he hasn't had a chance to unpack anything or settle in yet, so he might as well. He did say he'd talk to you about it in more detail."

"I'll reach out to him. We'll figure out what we need to do to get these guys out of here so we can figure out who they are and how to make them leave us alone, permanently."

"I'll settle for finding out who sent them and hopefully a little leverage to get them to back off."

They talked about details for a couple more minutes, then rang off. Ghost sat still a few moments, watching the assholes who were the reason he was out in the cold while he considered ways to get them to leave. What would make them go back to where they came from?

At the moment, Ghost didn't care if someone took their place as long as they went home, so he could follow. He sent a text to Malice and turned his mind back to how get these asshats to go home.

CHAPTER 5

Robyn stared at the building she'd just parked in front of and wished she didn't have to wait for it to open. She hated having to sit in the car, but it was better than standing in the freezing cold with snow over her ankles and more of it falling. It had been tempting to skip the grocery store this morning and just go home where she can be warm. But not only was she out of coffee, a nearly capitol crime in her books, but she was out of chocolate too. One or the other, she might have been able to live without, but both? Not a chance.

She checked her watch for what felt like the tenth time since she'd parked, less than five minutes before. Six more minutes until they opened. She rubbed her hands together and hoped the store would open early so she could get what she needed and get home.

Not for the first time, she wished she had given up coffee, but this time of year it was what kept her warm and moving, especially when she was on the night shift.

She had briefly considered getting enough of both from work to make it another day, but she'd spent the last half hour of her shift working on a grocery list, and there was more than she was willing to pay for from the convenience store where she worked. Besides, what she could get would cost as much as her entire list would at the grocery.

The morning manager, Bobby, unlocked the door, stepped outside, and looked around for a moment before going back inside. Robyn had been in enough just after opening that she'd learned who usually worked that shift. Taking Bobby's appearance as her cue, Robyn pulled up her scarf and headed inside. The faster she could finish her shopping, the faster she could get home and go to bed. For some reason night shift in the winter seemed to take so much more out of her than night shift during the summer.

She started at one end of the store and worked her way up and down each aisle, making sure she didn't miss anything on her list. It was an old-fashioned way to shop, but one she'd started when she was a child shopping with Mom, now it was habit and reminded her of Mom especially now that she wasn't around. She didn't see her mom as often as she once did. Not since she'd gotten married again and moved to Texas with her new husband. Robyn was happy for her mother, but that didn't mean she didn't miss her.

Robyn turned the corner and headed down the pasta aisle as she made a mental note to call Mom before work that evening. She wouldn't be up before Robyn went to bed, or if she was, she wouldn't be in any mood to chat. Robyn had learned to call in the afternoons or evenings if she wanted more than single syllable responses and grunts.

Robin's dad was different though. He would be up. She would call him on her way home.

She was almost done with her shopping, making her way through the produce section choosing the fruits and vegetables she wanted for the next week or so when a man approached.

He wasn't someone she knew, which wasn't all that uncommon in Dickenson.

"Where is she?" he demanded, acting like she should know who he was talking about.

"I'm sorry. Do I know you?"

He gripped both her upper arms and shook her.

"WHERE IS SHE?" he demanded again. He looked a few years younger than her, maybe twenty-four or twenty-five. His eyes were frantic, and Robyn fought to register more than the crazed look on his face, that he was yelling and shaking her.

Robyn opened her mouth to ask who he meant, but he cut her off, screaming in her face again.

"DON'T LIE TO ME. TELL ME WHERE SHE IS."

All Robyn could do was blink and wonder who he was talking about. Maybe it was a good thing he couldn't find her.

"Are you all right, Robyn?" Bobby's voice pulled her out of the shock of being shaken and having someone scream in her face.

"THIS BITCH WON'T TELL ME WHERE SHE IS." The man with a grip on her arms shook her again, not bothering to look up at Bobby, though he seemed to be talking to him. The longer the encounter went on, the more details she noticed. He wore jeans and a leather jacket. She could see the neck of some kind of white T-shirt underneath, but he wasn't dressed warm enough for the cold she'd come in from a few minutes ago.

"Who are you looking for, exactly?" Bobby's voice was calm, and Robyn could tell by the sound he was getting closer.

"You have to tell me where she is. I have to know." The volume in the stranger's voice dropped but his urgency didn't.

"Who are you looking for?" Robyn fought to keep her voice soft and calming, forcing her muscles to relax so she wouldn't fight his grip, no matter how badly she wanted to fight her way free. He was too close.

"I have to find her. Where are you hiding her?"

"I don't know who you're talking about. What's her name?" Robyn tried to get him to talk to her.

It seemed the more he talked, the calmer he got. His grip on her arms was tight enough it would probably bruise, but at least she wouldn't be seriously hurt.

She hazarded a glance toward where Bobby's voice had been coming from and saw him approaching carefully.

"Sir, who are you looking for?"

The stranger blinked but didn't look away from Robyn. His grip on her arms tightened.

"What did you do with her?"

"I don't know who you're talking about. What is her name? What is your name?" Robyn didn't know if the questions were helping, but he seemed to calm a little more with each one.

He blinked again, and his eyes seemed to focus on her face for the first time.

"I want to help you find her," Robyn kept her voice soft and soothing, "but I can't find her unless I know who we're talking about. What's her name?"

He finally seemed to understand what she was saying.

"Lili. Lili Mullins. Where is Lili?" He shook her as he asked the last, but not as hard as before.

"I don't know a Lili. Do you have a picture of her? Maybe I've seen her?" Robyn didn't know if it would help but it might get him to let her go. Especially if he had to reach for a phone or a photo.

"I know you have her." He shook her again.

Robyn fought to keep her head from snapping back and forth on her neck.

"I don't have anyone. I'm not hiding anyone but if you have a picture, I might have seen her." Robyn's gaze flicked to Bobby who was nodding, encouraging her to keep talking, at least that's what she thought he meant. "Do you have a picture?"

It seemed to sink in this time. "A picture? Yeah, I have a picture." The hands on her arms released as he reached for a phone, pulled it out and started flipping through photos.

"What's your name?" she asked again as he searched for a picture of the mysterious Lili.

"Me?" He didn't look away from the screen as he kept scrolling. "I'm Kyle."

"Hi Kyle, I'm Robyn. Have you found a picture of Lili yet?" She glanced back to where Bobby stood just out of the man's sight behind him. She wasn't sure if he didn't want to spook Kyle, was afraid of getting hit, or what. She was still watching Bobby when she saw a pair of police officers come around the corner and start down the aisle toward them.

"Here it is, here's Lili." Kyle's voice drew her gaze back to him. She looked down at the phone and saw a pretty girl, about his age, maybe a couple years younger, smiling at the camera, her arm around the man standing in front of Robyn now, though he looked a lot happier then.

Robyn glanced up to see where those police officers she'd seen a moment ago were. She didn't recognize the girl in the picture, but was afraid to say so for fear he'd grab her and start shaking her again.

"Is everything all right here?" one of the officers asked. Officer Carlson, according to his name plate, stepped between Robyn and the man. The young man looked up from where he was still looking at the photo on his phone, his eyes wide as he tried to figure out what was happening.

A hand wrapped gently around Robyn's forearm and tugged her away from the man. She turned to find Officer Bryan Dockter pulling her away. She didn't have to look at his uniform to know who he was. She'd grown up with him. She glanced back to make sure the stranger wasn't following, but the other officer seemed to have him under control.

Robyn turned back to Bryan and opened her mouth to ask if he knew who the stranger was, but he shook his head and pulled her farther down the aisle. She closed her mouth and followed. He led her around the corner until they were out of sight of the manager, the stranger, and the other officer.

"What happened here?" Bryan kept his voice soft, as if not wanting to alert the man who'd been shaking her where they'd gone.

"I'm really not sure. I was shopping, trying to get done and go home. I'm tired. I was thinking about my list and calling Dad on my way home and all of a sudden, this guy I've never seen before grabbed me and started shaking me while he screamed in my face."

"What was he saying?" Bryan pulled a small notebook from his shirt pocket, along with a pen and started taking notes.

"I think the first thing he said was 'Where is she?' He said that a couple times, then he accused me of lying about her, even though I don't remember saying anything."

"Is that all?"

Robyn looked at the floor and tried to remember what all had been said. "He shook me. He had a hold of my arms and shook me hard, trying to get me to tell him where Lili is. If I don't have bruises from his hands, it will likely only be because of how many layers I'm wearing."

"Tell me more about Lili. Have you seen her recently?"

"Not that I recall. I mean she's pretty and I might remember seeing her if she came through the station and got gas. Especially if she came inside and bought something, but unless there was something different about her visit than every other person who comes through, if I only saw her once I might not remember her. Hell, you know how it is this time of year with layers, scarves, and hats. I could have seen her a half dozen times and never be able to pick her out of a line up." She let out a mirthless laugh. "And I'm pretty good about faces. I might not remember her name in an hour, but I can usually remember a face if I've seen all of it."

"I know what you mean about hats and scarves. It makes identifying people difficult. What else can you tell me? Any little thing might help." Bryan fell silent as Robyn tried to remember the encounter.

At the time it seemed to take forever before the shaking had stopped and even longer until the stranger had released her but in reality, it probably hadn't been more than a few minutes. And now it all seemed to be a blur that was fading fast.

"He was frantic. He seemed to genuinely believe I was hiding her." Robyn looked up and met Bryan's gaze. "I have no idea why he thought it was me, was it my coat? My scarf? Something else? But he seemed sure I am keeping her from him. Do you have any idea who this Lili is?"

"I don't," Bryan said with a shake of his head. "But Carlson might after talking to him."

"I hate the idea of someone being missing. Especially around here when we probably know them or know their family. Let me know if there's anything I can do to help."

"Will do."

"How did you guys get here so fast?" Now that she thought about it, she was almost certain there hadn't been time for someone to call 911 and for them to get here, unless they'd been in the area.

One side of Bryan's mouth quirked upward. "You'll laugh." His face turned pink as he pressed his lips together and looked away.

Robyn watched him a moment, wondering what could be so bad to get such a reaction from him. "Come on, now you have to tell me. Besides, after that," she tilted her head toward aisle where the confrontation had occurred, "I could use a laugh."

He let his head drop until it hung for a moment then picked it up and glanced at her from the corner of one eye. "We were already here. We were getting donuts."

Robyn couldn't help but laugh. It was too cliché not to.

"Were you really?"

Bryan's face had turned pinker, he nodded. "We were. The chief has some meeting this morning and sent us to pick up a couple dozen for it."

She didn't even try to keep the grin off her face. "So, you were only handy to save my butt because a bunch of cops needed donuts?"

Bryan nodded. Keeping his gaze on the floor. "As much as it pains me to admit it, yes. I know you're not going to let that one go for a while."

"No. I'm not." She pressed her lips together in an effort to keep from laughing but she didn't laugh or pick at him about it. Not yet. She would wait until the time was right to make a dig at him about the cops needing their donuts.

It was tempting to say she gave up and would do her shopping later, but she didn't want to. She'd been almost done. Robyn took a deep breath and let it out slowly. How much longer would this take?

Just as she was about to say something, to complain about how long this was taking or crazy people interrupting her shopping, when Bobby came around the corner, towing her cart beside him.

"I'm really sorry about that, Robyn. I hope he didn't hurt you."

"Nothing serious." She was through talking about it. She wanted to finish her shopping and go home, and hopefully get to bed before noon. "Thanks for bringing me my stuff." She didn't want to look down the aisle to see if the stranger was still there because what if seeing her face set him off again? She went over what was down that aisle in her head, trying to decide if she needed anything there or if she could just skip it and move on.

After a few seconds she decided there was nothing down that aisle she needed bad enough to go back down there today, and after checking with Brian that he didn't need anything more from her, she hurried to finish her shopping and go home.

CHAPTER 6

Twenty-four hours after finding out Lurch hired Malice, Ghost and his old friend had the same men he'd been watching the day before in their sights, only now they weren't sitting beside the highway, waiting to harass the women coming and going from the Open A Bar T.

The two they were watching now had been replaced by another couple of idiots and it seemed the two he'd attached himself to were headed back to wherever they'd come from. Ghost was glad he didn't have to find a way to make them go back, but he wasn't going to let them get away either.

No. He and Malice were going to follow them back to whoever was giving the orders. The only way to get rid of the problem was to cut the head off the snake. And from as much trouble as they'd caused the Souls and the people surrounding them, this snake could be one nasty viper.

"I don't know how much Lurch told you, about these asshats and what they've been doing but they've been a big problem for the Souls." He glanced at where Malice sat in the passenger's seat of the pickup Ghost was driving. "You do know about the Demented Souls, right?"

"It's kind of hard not to know at least that they exist after spending more than an hour in the bunkhouse."

Ghost didn't have to be watching Malice to know he'd rolled his eyes as he'd spoken.

"I can tell you're a club, you seem to be a good bunch of guys, but something tells me there's more to your Souls than meets the eye."

Ghost shouldn't have been surprised. In reality, he should have expected

Malice to see beyond the surface and the cover that kept Ghost and the rest of his brothers safe. Or at least as safe as they could be with what they did. His buddy was usually pretty quick on the uptake, but Ghost had forgotten just how quick. He shot his old friend a look from the corner of his eye, but didn't say anything, at least not about his friend's suspicions.

"Did Lurch tell you why we're after these guys?" He didn't look at Malice to see if the other man noticed he was changing the subject, he would notice.

"He said they'd been causing trouble, but not how."

While they followed the other pick up at a distance that he hoped would be enough they wouldn't pick up that they were being tailed, but close enough not to lose them if they pulled off, he filled in his old buddy on what had been going on at the Open A Bar T. At least the parts he could share. He didn't tell him what the Souls really were or any of the things you had to be a member, or at least a prospect, to know about.

He had to be careful what he shared and how much, because he wanted Malice's help taking care of these shitheads, but he didn't want to get Lurch or Tuck on his ass or any of his brothers to end up dead because he shared too much. But who did he go to for how much he was allowed to tell Malice and whether or not they were willing to pull him in as a prospect, or possibly more?

If this had happened a few months ago, he would have no doubt. Tuck was the president of the Souls. But now that they were in the process of setting up a second home base here in Wyoming, Tuck couldn't be in charge of them both. Not with any efficiency nor a significant loss in efficacy.

With that in mind, Tuck had set things up here for the Gillette chapter with Lurch as the president. Despite Tuck's being stuck here for several more months, in order to satisfy the terms of the will that had given them their new base, Tuck had chosen to remain in charge of the original Tucson charter.

Ghost had a good idea of what Tuck would say, both about filling Malice in on what Ghost thought he needed to know and about Ghost's plan to take these fuck faces back to the source and put an end to the harassment once and for all; Lurch he didn't know so well. Though, since his girl Kerry was one of the women these fuck heads had been harassing, Ghost was willing to bet he'd get a green light.

Once he came up with a solid plan.

They'd been on the road maybe an hour when the Asshats' blinker came on. They were pulling off the highway. There was a large truck stop just off the highway and Ghost hoped that was where they were headed, at least as a first stop.

"I'm hoping they pull into the stop," he said to Malice. "If they do, you follow them inside, see what they're up to, use the facilities if you need to, you know how recon works, act natural and all that shit. I'm going to tag the truck with a tracker to make sure we don't lose them, then I'll be inside. Once that's done, we don't have to follow quite so close."

Malice nodded his head once, but didn't ask any questions. Once Malice had heard that these guys were harassing the women around the ranch, Ghost knew he'd been nearly as eager as the rest of the men to find out why.

It was one thing to have a beef with the club and to pester and harass them, but to take their issues to the women, who not only weren't expecting it but had nothing to do with club business? That was just too low. They had to make a stand and put an end to that shit.

While he hadn't been certain, Ghost had a pretty good idea that was how Malice would feel. It was only part of why he'd told him about it. His old friend needed to know what he was getting in to. Ghost had no doubt his old friend knew him well enough to know that once Ghost went after them, he would end it. One way or another

"Once we find out where they're from and who's calling the shots, then what?" Malice asked as Ghost maneuvered the vehicle off the interstate.

"I'm not sure yet. That is probably going to depend on who it is and why they're doing it." He didn't say it would also depend on what it took to make them stop.

They hadn't been on the road for a full two hours yet when they pulled into what looked like the biggest town they'd seen since Gillette. Most of the towns they'd passed through were little more than a wide spot with two or three houses.

"They stopped about a mile ahead of us, have been there about fifteen minutes," Malice said from where he was monitoring the tracker Ghost had put on the truck back at the truck stop. "Do we want to stop and wait for them to move again or what?"

"Let's cruise by and see what they're up to, then decide. We can't move on without them because we don't know which direction they will go from here. Logic says they'll continue north, but who knows?"

Malice glanced at him then back to the screen. "They're about a half a mile up, on the right."

Ghost didn't respond, just kept driving.

"There they are," Malice said a moment later. "Looks like they're filling up again. Didn't they just fill up?"

Ghost glanced down at the fuel gauge. They had barely used an eighth of a tank since they'd filled up outside of Gillette. But the idiots they were following had filled up when they'd pulled off the interstate at that truck stop. If they were filling up again, it most likely for one of two reasons... Either that pickup was a gas guzzler, which wasn't impossible, but more likely it was because wherever they planned to go, there wouldn't be gas available for a while.

"Yeah, and that means we better top off too."

"Not at the same station again?" It was Malice's tone more than his words that made that a question.

"Not if we can help it. I don't want them to see us too often and even suspect they're being followed. Besides, now that we've got them on a tracker, we don't have to keep them in sight."

Malice nodded as if he approved, but didn't say anything. They continued down the road until he spotted a little hole in the wall café that looked like it had been sitting there for half a century at least and may not have had a fresh coat of paint in all that time, but the parking lot was large and even at this odd hour for a meal, had a good number of cars scattered around.

"Let's find something to eat," Ghost said. "I don't know about you, but I'm getting hungry, plus it will give them time to do whatever they're doing in town and head out. We can follow their signal." He motioned to the monitor. "Plus, the less often they see us, the better."

Ghost pulled into the lot and parked. Malice shot him a look that said he wasn't sure he wanted to eat there, but kept his mouth shut as they climbed out and went inside.

Inside, the little restaurant looked better. It was clean and cared for, if a little aged. There were several empty tables, as well as several benches near the front, making Ghost wonder how long the wait to eat would be during normal mealtimes.

That was one thing about traveling, especially in the western states. You were limited to eating when you could find somewhere, and they were open. It led to people stopping when they could, instead of during mealtimes.

"Have a seat, anywhere you'd like. I'll be right with you," an older woman with blonde hair styled much like Ronald McDonald called out as she passed by, a full plate in each hand.

Ghost glanced at Malice to see if he had any preference, but his friend shrugged, so Ghost turned and led them to a corner where he could put his back to the wall and Malice could turn his seat so he could see the room.

They hadn't been seated more than a moment or two when the same woman as before appeared with two glasses of water and a pair of menus.

"Here you are, this will get you started. Can I get you something to drink to start you off?"

"Coffee, please," Malice said.

"No problem." She pulled a ticket pad from the pocket of her apron and turned to Ghost.

"Coffee."

"I'll be right back with that." She turned and walked away, not hurrying but moving quickly, as if that was how she moved all day.

Ghost turned his attention to the menu, but before he'd made it halfway through the first page, she was back, a pair of cups hooked over one finger, a bowl in the same hand and the coffee carafe in the other. She set the coffee pot on the table then laid the bowl down, it was filled with the little plastic cups of half and half, before setting cups in front of each of them and filling them from the pot she picked back up.

"I'll give you two a moment to look at the menu, but from the looks of it out there, I thought you might want some of this to warm up with." She gave them a kind smile then headed off to top off cups for some of the other tables before going back to the kitchen.

Ghost glanced across the table to Malice and found the other man watching her just has he had. He wasn't sure why, but something about her fit this place.

"I wonder what's good here?" Malice asked after a moment.

Ghost glanced around the room, at what other people were eating. There didn't seem to be any rhyme or reason, which usually meant all the food was good, not just a dish or two. "I wouldn't know, but I'm going to go with the western burger. It's probably not as hot as I'm used to, but green chili is green chili."

Malice shot him a brief scowl before turning back to the menu. "I'm thinking about a burger or maybe something else. A club sandwich sounds good too. And it's kind of hard to screw up."

Ghost quirked one corner of his mouth. "I get what you're saying but after hours in the truck staring at this mess," he tilted his head toward the window beside him, "I'm going to get something hot to eat. I get enough cold shit."

"The truck's warm."

Ghost nodded. "It is, at least now while it's running. But we may have some stake out time ahead of us, and I'm going to take the hot food while I can." He didn't mention the amount of time he'd already spent in the cold cab of the truck watching the fuckheads. He wasn't looking forward to more, but bitching about it would do no good either way.

Under an hour later they were back in the truck, gas topped off and following the dot that was their prey. They had left Belle Fourche a few minutes ahead of Ghost and Malice, and Ghost wanted to put eyes on them before they followed the electronic blip for eight hours in the wrong direction.

As soon as they were out of town and the speed limit increased to the usual highway limit, Ghost bumped his speed up.

"How fast does that thing say they're going?" he asked.

Malice was quiet long enough Ghost glanced at him to be sure he was looking for it.

"This thing says sixty-nine. I think they're hopeful it will happen. I've seen them. They shouldn't hold their breath."

Ghost rolled his eyes and ignored the commentary as he bumped his own speed up to almost eighty.

"Let me know when we're almost to them. I'll slow down a bit."

"All right." Malice kept his gaze on the screen for a few minutes then spoke up. "They're about a half mile ahead."

Ghost eased his foot off the accelerator, letting the truck slow naturally until they were still going a little faster than their prey, but not rocketing through the countryside. They slowed more as they got closer, giving Ghost a chance to check for oncoming traffic.

"It looks like the same truck, but make sure it's them as we pass," Ghost said as he hit his blinker and swung the pickup into the oncoming lane.

"It's them." Malice didn't twist in his seat or make it obvious he was watching the other vehicle as they passed. "But now we're in front of them, how will we know if they turn off?"

"If we were going to stay in front, we wouldn't, but I'm going to pull over in a couple miles, then wander off to one side of the road a ways, and let them pass us again. Then we'll keep our distance and wait to see where they end up. Then the real work will start."

Malice sat in the passenger seat, silent but watching. Ghost had forgotten that little thing about his friend. The silent unless he had something to contribute. He didn't mind, in fact, he was glad not to have one of the other men who never seemed to shut up long enough to hear anything but his own voice.

25

CHAPTER 7

I t wasn't until Robyn was sliding between the sheets, barely able to keep her eyes open that she remembered she'd planned to call Dad on her way home. She could do it now, but she was too sleepy. She'd talk to him tonight or maybe in the morning if she didn't remember before work.

After the drama of the morning, she'd been half afraid she wouldn't be able to sleep, but her head hit the pillow and she was asleep nearly faster than her eyes could drift shut.

T he phone ringing pulled Robyn out of a sound sleep. It took her a moment of groping and slapping at the table beside her bed to find her phone. The bedroom was barely lit, due to the blackout curtains she'd hung so she could sleep during the day, which didn't help when she needed to find something.

After what seemed like hours of a shrill ringing, she finally found the phone and turned it face up so she could hit the green button, then the speaker icon because she didn't want to hold it to her face.

"Hello?"

"Robyn, thank goodness." Her father sounded so relieved she sat up and stared at the phone. "Are you all right?"

"Yeah, I'm fine. I was sleeping. Has something happened?"

"I got a call telling me you'd been assaulted in Albertson's this morning.

They didn't know how bad you were hurt, and I hadn't heard from you in a couple days. I got worried."

A glance at the clock told her it was not yet noon. Robyn shook her head and wished the grapevine didn't move quite so fast. "I'm fine, Dad. I wouldn't have called what happened assault, but I guess it could be." She swung her legs off the side of the bed, stood and took her phone with her as she headed for the kitchen. It would take her a few minutes to reassure Dad and get him off the phone and she needed some water.

She recounted what happened as she went in the kitchen and filled a glass, then listened as Dad rambled while she drank more than half the water. Experience told her he would go on for a few minutes because he'd been worried then remember she'd been sleeping and let her go back to bed.

"Are you sure you weren't hurt?" His tone brought her back to the conversation.

"I'm sure. He held on to my arms and shook me. That's all. I might have bruises from his fingers tomorrow, but I don't think I will. I had on my coat. It's thick enough I shouldn't even bruise."

"I'm glad you weren't hurt. The way I heard it you'd been hit several times and were left bloodied and hurt."

Robyn shook her head. "You should know better than to listen to gossip, Dad. On the rare occasion they get something right, it's usually so blown out of proportion the story is unrecognizable."

"I know, but I didn't think that far. I had to check on you to be sure." His voice was calmer now, as if hearing her voice and talking to her for a moment had eased the worry and panic that had him forgetting she was on graveyards this week and would be asleep.

"I'm sorry you worried, Dad. I planned to call you on my way home, before all that happened. Afterward I was a little shaken and forgot. I got my groceries put away then I was so tired I crashed. I think I might have been asleep before my head hit the pillow."

"And I called and woke you up. I'm so sorry. I'll let you go back to sleep."

"Thanks for checking on me, Dad. I'll call tonight or tomorrow, and we can talk more."

"I'd like that."

She rang off, used the restroom, and went back to bed. Sleep didn't come quite so easily but it only took a few minutes before sleep washed over her.

Her alarm went off at 6:30, but Robyn had woken a few minutes before and lay in bed scrolling through TikTok when it went off. Reluctantly, she shut off the app, threw her blankets back and got out of bed. Winter was the worst time for getting out of bed because she hated stepping out of her warm blankets into the cold room, but why waste heat while she was in bed?

It wasn't as cold as it would be outside, she reminded herself as she stepped into her slippers and shuffled into the bathroom for a shower. At least she'd set the thermostat so it had started warming the place up about an hour earlier and by the time she got out of the shower it shouldn't be too cold. In her mind, programmable thermostats were one of the greatest inventions ever. It kept her from ever having to get up to freezing cold in the house, at least as long as the batteries hadn't died.

After her shower, Robyn called Mom, planning to chat while she dressed and got ready, but the call went to voice mail, so instead she called Dad back and caught up with him. After reassuring him again she was fine, and letting him know that no, she didn't have bruises, they moved on to other topics.

"Have you heard from your sister lately?" he asked.

"No, but that's not that uncommon." Robyn combed out her hair and sprayed in her leave in conditioner before leaving it to air dry while she finished her before work routine. She pulled on her jeans and shirt, then went into the kitchen, still wearing her slippers, because she needed coffee before much more thinking went on. With the coffee making she looked out the window to see if the forecasted snow had fallen while she slept. There was new snow, but it didn't look like the additional foot they'd been touting. Maybe six inches, if that.

"I talked to her a couple days ago. She has some news, but wants to tell you herself."

Robyn frowned. "You told her I'm working nights, right?"

"No, I forgot. I couldn't remember what you were working. She said she would text you to find out your schedule before she calls."

"I haven't heard from her yet." She couldn't help but wonder what Renea's news could be, or why she'd told Dad she wanted to tell Robyn herself, but hadn't reached out in two days.

"I'm sure she'll be in touch soon. When will you get a chance to come by? I've got a couple things I want you to see."

"Not for a couple more days. I'm not off until then and I'm just too tired to do more than work and sleep this time of year, especially on nights." She poured herself a cup of coffee and sipped it, closing her eyes while she waited for the dark brew to help kickstart her brain.

"Let me know when you have time to stop by. I'll let you go finish getting ready for work. Have a good night, hon."

"Good night, Dad, love you."

"Love you too." Her father disconnected the call.

Robyn stood in the kitchen drinking her coffee until she drained the cup, then poured another and took it back into the bedroom with her. She needed to finish getting ready for work, find something to eat, then head out and she was running out of time if she wanted to have time in case it took longer than usual to get there.

<h1 style="text-align:center">CHAPTER 8</h1>

I t was dark by the time the blip they'd been following through three states stopped. They were just outside the town of Dickenson, North Dakota and there was no way to know if they'd reached their final destination or it was a temporary stop. Even if they were done for the night, would they be traveling more tomorrow?

"Should we cruise by and see where they are? That might tell us something," Malice said as he watched the light where it sat still on the monitor.

"Can't hurt. There's been enough traffic on the road, they shouldn't recognize the truck, especially in the dark. But we'll need to find another vehicle if we're going to watch them."

Malice groaned. "I don't even want to think about sitting out in the cold trying to figure out what they're doing."

Ghost couldn't help the half smirk that lifted one side of his mouth. "At least we'll have the car. Last time you and I watched someone it was so cold it took me forever to get up from where I lay on the ground. I swear I was frozen to the rocks."

"That was only partly because of the cold. Partly because we'd lain there for two days."

"Don't remind me. I was trying to forget that part. I do my best to forget much of that time. Or at least the details of it. The lessons I keep with me. Those lessons I never want to forget."

Ghost kept his eyes on the road, but the glow from the tablet casting just enough light for him to catch Malice turning to stare at him a moment, then turn back toward the road. Ghost half expected his old friend to question him, or at least say something, but he remained quiet.

It took them a quarter of an hour to reach the town, then another ten minutes to get to where the dot they'd been following all day had stopped. Ghost was careful to keep the pickup at the speed limit as they cruised past the large building that looked like a warehouse with at least twenty bikes lined up outside. He didn't see much more than that as he let Malice do the looking for the both of them. They needed to look like any other car passing and slowing down so he could rubberneck would give them away if anyone was watching.

"Lots of bikes parked in the yard. My guess is this is either their club or an affiliate chapter where they knew they could find beds for the night."

"It's possible it's an affiliate, but I'm thinking it's more likely home. Why would they care about the Souls if they were from farther away? Hell, a full day's drive is far enough to wonder why they care about the Souls now."

"Maybe it's not about the Souls. Maybe it's about the land. Or maybe it's about Tuck. It could be one of a dozen things and without some clue, we may never know why they're harassing you guys."

At the next intersection, Ghost turned back toward the main road. They needed to find a place to stay at least for tonight if not for their whole stay.

Back on the highway, he found a motel with the entrances to the rooms on the outside walkway so fewer people might notice their coming and goings, then sent Malice in to acquire a pair of rooms while he deactivated the tracking beacon. He hoped that if whoever was in charge of security in the group these fuckwads were part of only did a bug sweep with an electronic detector, if they did that much. With the tracker deactivated, they wouldn't find it. If they did a visual inspection, it would be found but most people weren't as paranoid as the Souls were.

That reminded him. He'd have to walk Malice through the security protocols the Souls used before they went back to Wyoming. He'd use a modified version while they were here just in case his instincts had steered him wrong in bringing Malice into club business.

"I got us adjoining rooms. They only had a few options and I thought it might be more convenient if we want to talk or plan. We can open the doors, and no one will have any way to know," Malice said after he climbed back into the passenger's seat and pulled the door closed. A shudder ran through him.

Ghost nodded. "Good idea. I take it it's cold out there?"

"Fucking frigid. Makes me glad I packed my Thinsulate."

"I bet. I thought it was cold in Wyoming, but it will likely be even colder here." He eased the truck from the parking space beside the office, then turned to Malice. "Where's the rooms? Did you get ground floor?"

"Around corner on the far wing. I did, that's why there were two rooms together. Apparently, most people go for second floor rooms. From the way the clerk spoke, they'd rather haul the luggage than deal with people walking overhead."

"I'd rather have a heard of elephants in the room above me than have to jump from the second floor if I need to make a fast get away."

"That's what I had in mind."

Ghost steered the truck toward where Malice indicated, asked the room number, and found a parking spot only a couple spaces from the door. "You remembered the time we had to bug out of that dump we were camped out in the rock box, and we had to jump off the roof to keep from being caught by the insurgents coming up the stairs."

Malice shot him a glance as he twisted around to grab the duffel he'd left in the rear seat. "You know it." He handed Ghost a paper folder with a key card, lifted the bag over the seat, then opened the door and climbed down. "I'm gonna go inside and get settled. I'll open the door from my side, then you can open yours when you're ready."

The truck door slammed shut, leaving Ghost alone in the truck. With a sigh, he braced himself for the cold, then got out, retrieved his own duffle, and went in his room.

CHAPTER 9

Robyn had already finished her to do list, and cleaned up after the last group of people that had come in after shift change a little more than an hour ago. Now she sat behind the counter with her phone, reading on the library's Libby app. This was one of the few upsides to working the graveyard shift in the middle of the winter. Lots of time to read most nights.

The dual tones that indicate someone coming through the door pulled her attention from the screen. She looked up to find a tall guy wearing a knit cap pulled low on his neck wandering over toward the coffee pot. With his back to her she couldn't see much more about him other than that he was a foot or more taller than she was, but then at 5' 1" most of the world was taller than her.

"How fresh is this coffee?" a deep voice that stirred something in her belly asked.

She checked the clock, and silently told her hormones to calm the hell down before she answered. "I made it about twenty minutes ago."

He nodded then began fixing a cup.

"I'm not sure about anyone else's policy, but I never let a pot sit more than a couple hours. After that, I make a new pot."

"Good to know."

"You new around here?"

"I am. Not sure how long I'll be around, though. But it's always good to know where to find palatable coffee at all hours." He covered the cup with a disposable lid and turned to wander through the aisles.

Robyn couldn't help but watch him, though she tried not to be obvious about it. She didn't want him to think she was worried he was stealing or anything. It was just that there was something about him. Not just his voice, though that heat still pooled in her belly, making her wonder why she'd reacted like that.

As he turned up an aisle and headed her way, she got a look at his face, not that she could see much between the beard with a couple months' growth and the knit cap pulled down to his brows. What she could see made the heat in her belly grow even warmer and spread through her.

After a couple minutes, he brought the coffee and a couple candy bars up to the counter and slid them across.

Robyn was able to see his face better. His pale blue eyes intrigued her. She had to drag her gaze from his to ring up his purchases.

She couldn't help but give what she hoped was a friendly smile as she gave him the total and waited while he ran a card through the reader.

"Have a great night!" she said as he left.

"You too, and try to stay warm in here," his deep rumble of a voice came back as the door swung shut, cutting off the icy wind that had swirled into the small building as soon as he'd opened the door.

Robyn shivered a moment until the chill dissipated into the warmth of the room. She found herself staring at the door he'd left through, wondering if he'd been in before and she'd just not noticed him. How could you not notice those eyes?

Realizing she'd been staring blindly at the door for several minutes; Robyn shook herself and returned to her book. Sitting here mooning over a stranger who had barely said a dozen words to her yet had somehow stirred more sparks in her body in the five minutes he'd been in the store than her last boyfriend had in weeks, was foolish. She would probably never see him again. Not that she should care. Who picked up men in a gas station?

She didn't know how long she'd been staring at her phone thinking about the stranger, but her screen had shut off. Robyn shook her head and pushed him out of her mind. Instead of going back to her book she went to wipe up the counter where he'd made his coffee. It didn't need it, but it got her up and busy for a minute and she needed that. At least until something else came up to occupy her mind.

If it weren't so late, she would call Mom again. Maybe if she woke Mom up, she'd at least answer the phone... but it would be a conversation she was sure she would regret, so Robyn dismissed the idea.

Turning her attention back to her phone and the book she'd been reading, she tried to get back into the story. She gave up after reading the same paragraph four times and still not remembering what she'd read.

What she really needed was a distraction. She looked around the small building, looking for something, nearly anything to keep her mind from wandering back to the tall stranger whose voice did things to her she would be better off not thinking about.

CHAPTER 10

Ghost made it back to the motel less than twenty minutes after he'd left. He'd scouted the area to get an idea of what was around, then gone to the convenience store across the street and thankfully there wasn't enough traffic he'd needed to walk to the corner. After all day in the truck, he'd been glad to be able to walk over and stretch his legs a bit, but it was too cold to wander too far on foot. Especially at this hour.

He stepped into his room and closed the door, throwing the deadbolt before turning to the room, intent on stretching out on the bed, maybe turning on the TV while he drank his coffee and had his snack. Not that he was planning to eat both of the candy bars, but the price had been better to get two, and then he'd have one for tomorrow, or the next day. Whenever his sweet tooth struck again, because it wasn't a matter of if, but when.

"Still hooked on the sugar, I see." Malice's voice came from the shadowed corner next to the window.

Ghost clenched his teeth and fought not to jump and let the old man realize he'd startled him. He really should have noticed the other man in his room, but he'd been trapped in a truck with him for hours. Malice had become a normal part of his life again. A sometimes annoying one but still normal for Malice.

"I'll give up the sugar when I give up breathing."

Malice chuckled. "How have you not developed diabetes?"

"Healthy eating and clean, pious living."

Malice made sound like he was choking. Good. At least he still found Ghost amusing.

Ghost dropped the candy bars on the dresser beside the TV and peeled out if his winter gear. Hanging his coat on the back of the other chair that belonged to the small table next to the window where Malice still sat, then draping his pants over the seat, and set his boots on the floor under the heater to give everything a chance to dry out before he would need them again tomorrow. Not that they were very wet, not after the little amount of time he'd been out there. Still, it was a good habit to get into.

After he'd shed his outer layer, he proceeded to get comfortable. He stripped off his shirt and down to the insulating underwear he'd had on under his clothes, ignoring Malice as he grabbed a candy bar and the tv remote and stretched out on the bed.

"What's the plan?"

Ghost hit the power button and moved the candy bars to the night stand for now. "I'm going to find something to listen to and enjoy not having to bunk on a narrow cot for the first time in months while I figure out what kind of channels we get here. Not sure what you're going to do." He finally turned and looked at Malice. "Why are you still up and in my room at this hour anyway?" It was just shy of one in the morning.

"Pfft. This isn't late. I'm usually up at least a couple more hours."

Ghost scowled. Why would he be up until closer to dawn than the sunset?

"I was tending bar, remember?"

Ghost figured he must have looked confused. Which was fair.

"Sorry. It's been a long couple days and I admit, most of my attention has been on the asshats we followed up here. We'll see if they're still there tomorrow or if they hit the road again, then we'll decide what our next move will be."

"I guess I'll have to live with that." Malice motioned to the TV with his chin. "What you planning to watch?"

Ghost turned his attention back to the TV and turned it on. "I don't know. I have no idea what's on. The crowd at the bunk house told me I get the TV without competition in the early mornings, so they get to control it in the evenings. They rarely have it on any kind of programming. One or another is usually playing some kind of game."

"Still not into video games."

Ghost shook his head, his attention back on the screen as he flipped through the onscreen guide to see what was on. "Still don't see the draw. That's probably not going to change. But you'll find people to play with once we're back at the ranch."

"We'll see." Malice shrugged then slouched in his seat, propping his sock-clad feet up on the far side of Ghost's bed. "Most gamers are into multi player action games, at least most of the ones who game socially. I'm more into longer adventure/puzzle games. We'll see if anyone else plays what I'm into."

"And if they're not?"

"I'll find time to play on my own. Not sure how we'll work it out until I get down there. Who knows when that might be. We've got to take care of this here first."

"Here or wherever we end up being. This may simply be an overnight stop. We have to be prepared for that."

"I am. I did a bit of research. From here they can go either direction on the 94, but unless they're headed anywhere but a few places, there are easier, faster routes. They could keep going north. There are a few towns, but they're smaller than this one. Unless they're headed north of the border, but again, there are faster and easier routes. I think they were headed here specifically, whether as a stopping point or a destination. The question either way, is why?"

"The why is probably in that warehouse. It only becomes a question if they keep moving tomorrow. If they stay in town, then it's likely the HQ of whatever group sent them after us. Then the question is still why, but more about the group than why stop here."

Malice fell silent for a few minutes as Ghost continued to watch the screen, then turned the channel to a movie he'd seen at least a dozen times but at least it was something to listen to that wasn't going to irritate the shit out of him like grown men bickering over video games.

With what he'd watch, or rather listen to, settled, Ghost dropped the remote on the bedside table and picked his coffee back up and took a sip. He closed his eyes and let the flavor wash through his senses, relaxing him as much as that first cup in the morning woke him. Ghost stayed that way a couple moments, letting some of the tension from driving all day and being on the lookout for the fuckwads they'd been following, drain from his body.

When he opened his eyes, he glanced to where Malice still sat in the shadowed corner of the room.

"You going to sit there all night?"

"I was considering it, if only to see how far I can push you before you start snarling at me."

That made Ghost turn and stare at him. One corner of Malice's mouth quirked up, letting Ghost know his buddy had gotten the reaction he'd hoped to. He slowly shook his head as he turned back to the TV and his coffee, determined to ignore Malice's attempts to get on his nerves. He'd forgotten that little quirk of his old friend. Now that he did remember it, he also recalled the best way to deal with it was to ignore it. Eventually, if he didn't get a reaction, Malice would drop the digs, Ghost could only look forward to when that happened.

T he sun was up and shining in the window when Ghost woke the next morning. He blinked, then sat up and looked around. More light than he'd expected poured through the curtain. He could barely believe it was he'd slept so long. He hadn't slept that late in months. Hell, he hadn't been up after the sun since he'd left Arizona. Not that the sun came up later there, it was actually a few minutes earlier, but his schedule had changed when working on the ranch and they were up before the sun came up so they could be ready to use the daylight to get what they needed to done.

He flipped the blanket back and swung his legs over the edge before bothering to look for a clock. After eight. When was the last time he'd slept past seven? He couldn't say for sure, but it had been a while. Shaking his head in disbelief, he picked up the tablet hooked to the tracking device and checked on the location of the truck they'd been following. They were still at the warehouse he and Malice had tracked them to the night before.

Ghost let out a sigh of relief that they didn't have to scramble to get moving or spend another day on the road, then pushed himself to his feet and shuffled into the bathroom.

Fifteen minutes later, Ghost stepped out of the bathroom to get dressed.

"Jesus. Put some clothes on!"

"You know, if you weren't sneaking into my room when I've got the door between the rooms closed, then you wouldn't have to worry about seeing my naked ass." Ghost knew better than to yell about the other man sneaking in, it was just another way the other man irritated people in his seemingly endless ploy to drive them out of their minds.

Ghost didn't understand the odd thrill Malice seemed to get out of driving people out of their minds with stupid shit, only that he did. Ignoring the intruder in his room, Ghost pulled out his clothes and dressed. His time in the military had long since stripped him of any worry about people seeing him without clothes.

"What's the plan for today?" Malice asked as Ghost sat to pull on his socks and boots. His partner sat in the same chair he'd been in the night before, fully dressed, even down to his boots.

"I was thinking I'd go next door and get something for breakfast. After that, we'll see."

"Can I come or am I on my own?"

"You're welcome to join me."

"What about the guys we followed up here?"

"They're still at the warehouse, or at least the truck is. I checked before my shower."

Malice stared at him a long moment, then blinked and stared a moment longer. "I'd feel better if we did a drive by before we ate, just to make sure the truck is still there. That they didn't find the tracker and leave that there while they've left town."

Malice was right, Ghost knew it. He hated admitting it. It only made Malice more difficult to live with, at least it had before Ghost had left the Marines.

Maybe he'd gotten better over the last few years. A glance at Malice told Ghost enough to believe his buddy hadn't changed that much. He could tell from the single lifted brow and smug smirk Malice wore.

"If we're going to go check on the truck, we can go anywhere. I was just going to go next door to eat because it's close and convenient. Is there somewhere else you'd like to go?" Ghost stood and finished gathering his things, putting on his belt and the holster he wore in the small of his back, he put the holster in place before shoving his knife and phone into his pockets and picking up the tablet, checking again to make sure the truck hadn't moved in the last half hour.

The indicator light showed the truck had moved since he'd last checked it, but it was actually closer to them now.

"They've moved, but not far."

"Oh? If they didn't go far, I take it they're not still on the move?"

"Not according to this." Ghost handed the table to Malice then picked up his jacket and pulled it on. "You ready?" He took the cap from the table where he'd left it the night before and tugged it on, pulling it down low to cover as much of his ears as he could.

"I just need to grab my coat." Malice pushed himself to his feet. "I'll meet you out at the truck in just a minute."

Ghost watched as Malice disappeared through the door adjoining the two rooms, then once again, turned the deadbolt on the door between them. He knew it wouldn't stop Malice from coming and going as he pleased, but it would keep housekeeping from knowing they were going back and forth. Though ghost wasn't sure why that was so important to him. He trusted his gut that it was though.

With one last glance around the room, making sure he hadn't left anything out that might be taken as suspicious or used against him, Ghost double checked his jacket pocket for the room key, then let himself out and headed for the truck.

An icy wind hit him in the face as he stepped outside, sending a shiver through him. He pulled the door shut then tested to make sure it had latched before going to the truck, climbing inside, and starting it. Malice hadn't stepped out yet, but the truck would need to warm up for a couple minutes before the heater did much good. At least there wasn't new snow that he'd have to clean off before they could leave. Though the dark clouds over head threatened more snow to come. He just hoped he could hole up in the room and wait for it to pass. But that meant they needed to get their business done and a little additional shopping before the storm broke.

Thirty minutes later, Ghost pulled the truck into the parking lot of a little local diner with nearly a dozen cars in the lot. He was glad they'd gone looking for the truck, not because they'd found that they'd ditched the tracker, they hadn't, but more because it proved Ghost had been right. The men they'd been following were coming out of a convenience store as they drove past, confirming not only was the tracker still where they'd left it, but that the men were still with the truck. It left him feeling good, but he didn't say anything. It would only make him feel like he was stooping to Malice's level.

Instead, he climbed down from the truck and went into the diner. This place had more vehicles parked outside than the Denny's he'd been planning on. He hoped that meant the food was better.

He stopped just inside the door and looked around.

"Good morning," a cheerful voice called, "have a seat. I'll be right with you." A woman stepped around a corner, a half apron around her waist and a tray of drinks in one hand. She smiled at them. "Any open seat is fine."

Ghost nodded, glanced around the room again then headed for a table. When he got to the table near one wall, he slid into the seat against the wall, giving him a good view of the entire place. He hated having his back to the room and couldn't help the burst of satisfaction that went through him that he's managed to stick Malice with that seat this time.

Almost as soon as they'd sat the waitress appeared, a coffee pot in hand. "Coffee?"

"Please," Ghost flipped the cup on the table over. Malice did the same.

She poured the hot brew with ease born of practice, then set a couple menus on the table.

"I'll give you a moment to look these over then I'll be back." She hurried off, filling cups as she made her way back to the counter, her pot nearly empty by the time she set it back on the warmer.

The waitress had returned, taken their order, and disappeared again before Malice spoke to him.

"You were right, they're still in town. What's the plan next?"

Ghost scanned the room, then decided there was no one near enough to overhear them. "First, we need another vehicle or some kind of shelter to watch them from. We also need to figure out who's in charge of the group, because from the size of that warehouse and the number of bikes in front, there is a leader." He shook his head, still finding it hard to believe how many bikes had been parked out there. Especially with the biting cold that he was sure wouldn't lift for months. Who rode in these temperatures?

"And then?"

"Once we know who the leader is, that might help us find out why these asshats are harassing us and our women. Or it might not. We may have to do a little more investigative work."

"Investigative work?" Malice didn't seem sure about investigation.

What Ghost wasn't going to say here, where anyone might overhear them, is that 'investigative work' might include some questionably legal activities, including but probably not limited to breaking and entering as well as possibly some kidnapping and creative questioning techniques.

Ghost nodded and sipped his coffee. He hadn't been thrilled with waiting nearly an hour after getting up for coffee, and he might have to invest in a thermos to fill at that convenience store across the street in the evenings so he could have hot coffee in his room in the mornings.

A thermos would be handy for stake outs too... for while they were trying to figure out who was in charge of this circus. He wished for a moment he'd thought to bring one from the ranch.

"What kind of investigative work?" Malice wasn't going to let it go.

"The kind this isn't the place to discuss." Ghost met Malice's gaze for a moment then looked away. "We need to figure out where to pick up a cheap vehicle. Preferably one the heater works in."

Malice stared at him a moment then pulled out his phone and started tapping on the screen. Ghost watched people in the diner. There were a couple of larger groups of people, one of older men, chatting, laughing, and drinking coffee. His guess from watching them was they could probably be found in exactly those seats several days a week. The other larger group looked like a family, three or four generations, probably out to celebrate some special event on their way through town on a trip.

There were a few people scattered through the place at other tables, some alone, others in pairs. Most were busy eating, some talking, but there was one pair, two men much like he and Malice, both were eating and staring at their phones. Ghost had to wonder why they were there. Were they traveling through and just needing a meal? Something else? After being in the truck all day, and still being in need of more caffeine to jump start his brain, Ghost wasn't in the mood to talk much either, especially to the man who kept turning up in his room at inconvenient moments.

Not that he was pissed at Malice, just annoyed with him, and knew that if he tried too hard to be friendly, it would come out wrong and only encourage his partner to be even more irritating.

"What's the budget?" Malice's words brought Ghost's attention back to him.

"Budget for what?"

"For a vehicle."

"Oh. I guess it depends on what it is. We want to make sure it blends in. I'd be willing to pay more for a pickup than a car, and more for four wheel drive than two."

Malice gave him a half lidded stare that Ghost knew was him asking if Ghost thought he was an idiot.

"I know how to watch people. I know it has to blend. How much of a beater do you want?"

"How much of a not beater can we get away with in that neighborhood? You were able to see more of it than I was. I was focused on the road."

Malice frowned at him a moment then turned his attention back to the phone without another word. Ghost didn't know if that was because he didn't know what to say or what he wanted to say was better not said here.

When the waitress brought out their food, Malice laid his phone face down on the table and they ate.

⚜

After their meal, when they'd gotten back in the truck Malice brought it back up.

"The neighborhood where the warehouse is had a good variety when it came to ages of the pickups in the area. We could go with any thing from five to forty years old, and neither would look too out of place as long as it isn't beat all to hell. As for what's available even somewhat locally, and at what cost, that's a different story."

Ghost started the truck and backed out of the parking space without looking at Malice. "Go on." He glanced at the tablet he'd set on top of the console to get an idea of where he was going before pulling out onto the street.

"What is available depends on a couple factors."

"Like?"

"First is private owner or dealership. From the age of what we're looking at, I'm going to guess we're wanting something from a private owner." Malice paused, looking at Ghost for confirmation.

"Private is my preference. Though we can go through a dealership if we find a better deal."

"All right, good to know. Second factor is distance. How far are we willing to go to find this truck?"

Ghost took a deep breath and thought about it for a moment or two. "It would be best if we don't get one here in town. Less chance it will be recognized. But I'd rather not go more than hour or two away. Too much can change in the time it would take to make the trip and back to get it."

"Good point. Third factor. I assume you're looking to pay cash. I need to know what's the upper limit of what you're willing to spend on this so I can keep inside what we have access to."

"Unless we're looking to spend fifty thousand, I can cover it in cash. I'll have to hit a bank and see about a cashier's check, but I can do it."

Malice stared at him a moment, his mouth hanging open. "The ranch has that much ready cash?"

"I don't know what the ranch has available, but I can get it. I'll worry about reimbursement later, or I may end up keeping the truck for myself it if I like it."

"I thought this was yours." Malice looked around the cab of the pick-up, they'd spent more time in than out of in the last twenty-four hours.

Ghost eased up to a light then made a right turn toward the little blue light on the screen between them. The gray skies that had been threatening more snow since he'd stepped foot outside this morning had started giving flurries here and there. Nothing heavy yet, but from the looks of the clouds, it was just a matter of time.

"Nah, this belongs to the ranch. I left my truck in Tucson. It's older and only two-wheel drive. I could probably get by with it up here, but I've been considering picking up something a little more fitting for while I'm up here."

"All right," Malice said as he gave a slow nod, as if he understood all the words, but thought there was something not quite right about them.

"Keep an eye out for the truck. We're getting close to that dot." Ghost watched his side of the road as he tried to keep from looking like he was searching for something and drove down the narrow residential street.

"There it is. In that driveway."

"Good. Anyone around? See one of our assholes?"

"Nope. But I wouldn't be standing out in the cold to watch for people driving by. Not in this weather."

"Good point. Now that we know where the truck is, find me a Walmart or Target. One that's either got a grocery store in the building or nearby would be a plus."

"No problem."

CHAPTER 11

Robyn's alarm woke her at 6:30 that evening. The same time she always got up for a night shift. It wasn't until she was dressed and headed for food that she looked outside.

"Son of a bitch," she muttered to herself when she spotted the additional four inches of snow on her porch.

It wasn't the snow, she didn't mind the snow all that much, at least not this early in the season. But looking farther down the road she could see they hadn't kept up with it on her street, which meant she'd need more time to get to work. That did annoy her.

She liked her quiet time to mentally prepare for her day, and hated having to spend that on the road, dealing with ice, snow, and idiot drivers. Still scowling, Robyn made her way into the kitchen to get something to eat, and more coffee. If she had to leave early because of the weather and roads, she was definitely going to need more coffee.

It took Robyn longer than usual to get to work that evening, but not longer than she anticipated, so she made it in plenty of time. By eleven, the evening crowd, or what little of it appeared to be coming through tonight, had gone. She still had a little cleaning up to do, but would wait to do it or she'd end up having to redo it several times if she cleaned up after each person that came in. The floors were a little grimy from the snow and ice people had tracked in, but it wasn't bad, and she'd already gone through with the mop and cleaned up any pooling water, so it wasn't a slip hazard. Sometime around three she would clean them again.

Now she sat with her book, trying to force herself to focus on the story, and not that stranger's voice from last night. She was succeeding, losing herself in the story until the bell for the door rang, yanking her from the story. Her heart thundered in her ears as she looked up.

Robyn couldn't help the disappointment that crashed through her when she spotted the woman who had just stepped inside. But she plastered a smile on her face and greeted her anyway. There was no way she'd let this customer know she was disappointed to see her.

Mentally, she shook her head at how ridiculous it was to hope to see someone who had only come in once before.

The woman chose her purchases and brought them to the counter.

"It's really coming down out there. They're forecasting another six inches before morning."

Robyn nodded. "I'd heard that. Someone came in earlier and said if it gets much worse, they may close roads until morning."

"That will mean delays in the morning and traffic, what there is of it, will be miserable."

"And I'll either be totally dead in here or hopping busy. You can never tell which way it will go." Robyn finished bagging up the purchases while the woman paid for them.

"Have a good night." The woman took her bags and left, leaving Robyn alone again. She noticed the coffee pot didn't have enough in it for another cup, so she made a fresh pot then went back behind the counter and picked up her phone, planning to start reading again, but instead opened a game.

She'd lost track of time as she played the game, at first passing a couple levels, then getting stuck on a hard one and trying several times before being able to beat it. She was half way through the next level, feeling pretty good about her progress when the alarm for the door went off again.

"Welcome, hope you're having a good evening," she said without looking up, as she was engrossed in the level she was trying to beat.

"So far so good, but it's a little late to be considered evening."

The deep rumble of that voice shot straight to her lower belly, making it do somersaults and warm. Robyn closed her eyes, gripped the phone in her hands tight and took a deep breath. Why did this stranger affect her so strongly? Was it something about him? Something about her? She didn't know. What she did know was she liked the way he made her feel, even if she didn't quite understand it.

"Hey," she tilted her head up and smiled at him, "you're still in town."

"Yeah, it looks like I may be here a little while, at least." He was fixing himself another cup of coffee, then filling a thermos she hadn't seen him bring in. "I hope you don't mind I'm taking all your coffee."

"Not at all. That's what it's there for."

He glanced in her direction then looked back at what he was doing. Once the thermos was full, he put the carafe back on the warmer and flipped the power switch as if it was automatic. After finishing up at the coffee station, he wandered through the shop a moment more before bringing his coffee and a couple other items to the counter.

"How's that place across the street for breakfast?"

"It's all right. I've been there a couple times and it's not bad."

"Is there somewhere else you prefer?"

She scowled and wondered for a moment if he was hitting on her.

"Like I said last night. I'm new in town. I'm just looking for decent places to get food. I learned a long time ago the best way is to ask locals."

Robyn's smile returned. "That's smart. I'm not really big on breakfast's out but there's a place down on Villard, near Tenth. That's my favorite for breakfasts."

He looked out the glass door at where the snow still fell in huge flakes that she knew walking or driving through would make it look like warp speed in Star Wars.

"Looks like I may not get to try it tomorrow, but who knows, this might hold me over until they get the roads plowed." He motioned to the thermos.

"That's a good plan. I take it you're staying over there?" she tilted her head toward the motel next to the restaurant he'd asked about earlier. "Don't they have coffee makers in the room?"

"They do, but who knows how often they're cleaned or what anyone has put through them. I never trust the in-room coffee makers in a motel." He grinned at her. "Besides, filling up on coffee for morning and my sweet tooth give me an excuse to come see you."

Robyn's face heated. He was flirting with her. "I don't mind."

"I'm glad. You work tomorrow too?"

Her mind raced. Was there any reason she shouldn't tell him? As far as she knew there was no one out to get her, and she wasn't worried about her safety, not with the cameras through out the building, inside and out. Besides, half the police in town stopped in here to get coffee just like he was doing. They all knew her schedule too and if something were to happen to her, they'd know sooner than anyone else.

"I do. I guess I'll see you then?"

"If I don't see you before then, I'll probably see you tomorrow."

She couldn't help lifting one brow and grinning at him. "Think you'll need more coffee than a full thermos before I get off in a few hours? You stay up all night too?"

"Not deliberately, but sometimes I have a hard time sleeping, and if I do, I may need more sugar." He tilted his head toward the candy bars on the counter.

Robyn laughed. "Not that I don't want to see you again, but I hope you sleep well. Not being able to sleep is miserable and I only have a few enemies I'd wish that on."

His eyes narrowed. "You have enemies? Somehow, I find that hard to believe."

"I do. They may not know I'm their enemy, but that's how I see them."

"Do I need to ask who? The last thing I want is you to get hurt."

Robyn waved one hand through the air.

"No one who even knows I exist. I'm in no danger."

"I'm glad to hear it." He picked up his candy and stuffed it in his pockets, then took his coffee and thermos. "I guess I'll see you tomorrow then, unless I have trouble sleeping."

"I'll see you tomorrow." She smiled and watched him go.

After he walked out, she watched as he made his way carefully across the street, until the falling snow made him disappear before he made it to the motel building. Once she could no longer see him, she went back to the stool where she'd been sitting, but didn't bother to pick up her phone. Instead, she wondered what it was about this guy that called to her. Why she found herself waiting to see him? Why he made her body react like it did?

She didn't have the answers to any of her questions, and she didn't know how to find them. But she did have seeing him tomorrow to look forward to. She'd have to live with that for now.

CHAPTER 12

Ghost let himself back into his room, mentally cursing the storm that blew the small crystals of ice into his face no matter which way he turned. Remembering the night before, he checked the corner for Malice as he turned to thumb the dead bolt, then turning back to the room. He ignored his old spotter as he set his cup and thermos on the table and started peeling out of his outdoor gear.

"More coffee? Are you planning to sleep tonight?"

"Of course, I am. Coffee only keeps me up if I want it to."

"I don't thing the science of that works the way you think it does."

"I don't give a shit about the science of it. I know how my brain works. I can drink coffee and stay awake. I can drink coffee and go to sleep."

"Where did you find a place to fill the thermos? The office?"

"Nope, that gas station across the street. Same place I got tonight's cup." He pulled the candy out of his pockets and put it on the table with the coffee before shedding the coat and hanging it up like last night.

"You and the sugar." Malice shook his head but didn't move to leave.

Ghost could deal with that. He ignored the other man, for the most part. It was the only way to deal with the endless picking.

Once he'd stripped his outer wear, Ghost gathered the thermos and coffee cup and took them farther into the room. He deposited the thermos next to the coffee pot he refused to use, and the cup on the table beside the bed. Then he went back and gathered the candy to add to the stash of food in the room. He'd intended to get his candy when they'd been at the store earlier, but he'd forgotten while they'd been more focused on the rest of the food that they would likely want over the next few days with the storms moving in.

"Have you checked on the assholes recently?" Ghost asked as he picked up the remote and turned on the TV.

"I checked while you were off supplying your caffeine addiction. The truck is back at the warehouse."

"Good. At least we know they haven't left town again."

"What's the plan then?"

"Have you found a truck yet?"

"I've found a few good leads. Tell me which you'd prefer." He pulled out his phone and started going over details of the trucks he'd found for sale. Ghost listened while he flipped through the guide on the TV, trying to find something to listen to.

"What are the colors?"

"The Ford is red, the GMC is white, and the Toyota is green."

"What shade of green?"

Malice was silent a moment, tapping at and messing with his phone, "It looks like OD green. Why would they make a car that color on purpose? It must not have sold well. I don't remember seeing any on the road."

"Either that or it did it's job and camouflaged itself and you just don't remember it. Either way I don't think so on that one. And no on the red. The white sounds like our best bet. Was that one four-wheel drive?"

"They all were. This one is the 2500 HD, so it's got a bigger engine, lifted, more of a work truck than a fancy tricked out truck."

"Perfect. Sounds like exactly what I'm looking for. What kind of condition does it say it's in?"

"Very good. Which means it is mechanically sound, maybe some small cosmetic dings or touchups."

"I know what very good means." Ghost didn't bother to shoot Malice a dirty look for explaining what he already knew. "Is that a dealership or a private owner?"

"Dealership. In Bismarck."

"Ok, send them an email inquiring. Tell them we're looking to pay cash, offer ten k below the listed price. Let's see what they say." He had no doubt they would refuse it, but it was a starting point. He really wanted to get the truck for five thousand under what they were asking, but if he could get them to take seven thousand off, he'd take that too. He settled on a History Channel docudrama and tuned in. It wasn't real but it was entertaining.

"Is that all?"

"All what?"

"All the plans?"

"We'll wait to see what they say in the morning. It's too late for them to respond tonight, and even if they did, we can't make it over there until tomorrow. No point in waiting up to negotiate farther."

"That's not what I meant."

Ghost turned from the TV and stared at Malice a moment. "You can take the truck out, sit outside that warehouse in the storm if you want, but you won't be able to see much, if anything. Hell, you can't even see the gas station across the street for the snow falling."

Malice pulled one side of the curtain away from the window and looked out.

"It's coming down out there. How much are we supposed to get tonight?"

"I don't know. Don't care either. I'm prepared in case they close the roads. But if they don't and we can make the deal on that GMC, we'll probably be going to Bismarck tomorrow."

His phone ringing woke Ghost the next morning. A glance at the screen told him it was Lurch.

"Hello?" he asked without bothering to get out of bed or sit up.

"Morning. Found anything yet?"

"Nothing I haven't already reported. We're in North Dakota, small city called Dickenson. It's close to the size of Gillette, maybe a little smaller. These assholes have been mostly holed up at a warehouse that had maybe twenty bikes lined up outside the night we got here. That's got to be a clubhouse, but I haven't figured out what the club is yet. They've gone a couple other places in town but as of just shy of midnight last night they were back at the warehouse."

"Are you keeping eyes on or tracking them?"

"Just tracking and checking in on so far. I'm afraid they'll recognize the truck I'm in, either from when they were watching the ranch or from it being around their clubhouse too often. We're working on getting another pickup, one that will blend in better. On top of that, it's been storming. The snow was so thick last night we couldn't see across the street from the motel. Sitting on the street all night would have given us no usable intel, and frozen my ass off."

"I'm not complaining, just wanted to know. I trust you to get the job done." Lurch fell silent for a moment.

Ghost turned toward the window, there was no light leaking around the drapes, it must be pretty early.

"You said you were looking to buy a truck. Do you need help with funding for that?"

"I can cover it. Once this job is done, we can talk about if we want it for a ranch truck and the ranch wants to buy it off me or if I want to keep it, but I can cover it for now."

"If that's what you want to do. Let me know if you need anything from us. Information, money, help in any way we can give it. I'll do my best to get you what you need."

"We're good for now. I'd really love it to stop snowing. For a day or two at least, but we'll deal with what we get."

"How are things going with the new guy?"

"Fine. Nothing surprising. I've worked with him before and knew we would work well together. I'd forgotten some of his more irritating habits, but we're doing fine."

"How's he doing on the job?"

"I have no complaints."

"You think he'll end up patching in?"

"Not sure. We haven't talked about it all. He may end up staying a ranch hand or even moving on. I'll have to spend more time with him, work with him longer to get a better read on him now. It has been a long time since I'd worked with him before, and things can change over time. Though, his tendency to make me want to throttle him at times hasn't changed all that much." Ghost fell silent as he tried to find the right words. He turned to look at the clock on the nightstand on the other side of the bed from the window. 6:48 a.m. "I wouldn't have recommended him if I didn't think he would be a good fit, not just for the ranch, but for the Souls too."

"Good to know. Let me know if there's anything you need or if you find out anything important."

"Will do." Ghost rang off, dropped his phone back on the nightstand and lay staring at the ceiling; the room wasn't completely dark like it had been the night before, so the sun was starting to come up. He lay a moment longer, considering whether or not he should go back to sleep, or if he even could. After a few minutes, he decided to just get up. Might as well get on with his day.

As he shuffled into the bathroom, he couldn't help but wonder what time that cute girl from the gas station got off work.

That morning as Robyn left the convenience store, she made her way out to her car, opened it up, started it, and pulled out the snow brush. As she was cleaning the night's snowfall off so she could go home, her mind turned back to the stranger.

She looked toward the motel he'd said he was staying at, but no one seemed to be stirring, though it was difficult to see much with only the street lights lighting the area, as the sun was just starting to rise. He must have been able to sleep because she hadn't seen him after he'd filled the thermos.

It wasn't that she wanted him to have trouble sleeping, but she'd kind of hoped to see him again. Shaking her head, she went back to cleaning off her car. The sooner she finished the sooner she could get in the car and out of the cold.

A few minutes later, she'd cleared off the nearly six inches that had fallen since she'd gotten to work the night before. She didn't know how much had been forecast for the night, but she didn't think it was this much. Not that it mattered. It was here and that was all that mattered. She cleared the last of the snow off the back of her car, then got inside.

She tucked the brush back where it belonged and sat for a moment enjoying the warmth that had built in the car while she'd worked. After a minute or two she opened the front of her coat so she wouldn't overheat, then buckled her seatbelt, put the car in gear and headed home.

Whil Robyn got home, she parked on the street, went inside long enough to fetch her shovel then came out and cleaned the new fall off her driveway and walkway before it melted and turned to ice. When she'd finished her own, she went to work on her next-door neighbor's walkway and driveway. Not that Mrs. Morgan would be driving. Her neighbor was somewhere north of eighty and she'd given up her car a couple of years ago. But her son and daughter would need to get into the driveway to take her out. Having the driveway clear would make it easier for them and help keep Mrs. Morgan from falling.

She was just finishing up her neighbor's walkway and steps when Mrs. Morgan opened the front door.

"Robyn, you're such a sweetheart. I was wondering how I'd get that all shoveled before Sarah comes to pick me up this morning."

"I was doing mine and thought I'd get yours taken care of real quick. I didn't want it to start melting. That makes it so much harder to clear."

"It does. Let me pay you something for your trouble." Mrs. Morgan stepped away from the door as if going for her purse. Robyn knew it would do no good to call after her, so she waited until the elder woman returned to the door, cash in hand, then refused.

"I don't need it. I didn't do it for you to pay me. I did it because it was no trouble."

Mrs. Morgan would hear nothing of it, so rather than keep arguing, Robyn took the folded cash the older woman tucked into her hand, planning to watch for Sarah to arrive so she could give it back. "What time is Sarah coming to get you this morning?"

"My appointment is at eleven. She's supposed to get her at about ten to make sure I'm ready." Mrs. Morgan shook her head. "I can get ready by myself."

"I'm sure you can. Maybe she just wants to spend some time with you."

Mrs. Morgan was quiet a moment, then tilted her head. "I would like to spend some time with her too."

"It's cold out here. You go back inside and keep warm. Have a good visit with Sarah."

"I will. You go inside too, dear. Warm up and sleep well today. I hate you working all night then driving in the snow like this."

"I'm used to working at night. But the snow isn't my favorite either. Have a good day!" Robyn watched as Mrs. Morgan went inside and closed the door then she took her shovel and went home. She put the tools away, then moved her car from the street to the driveway and went inside. She'd spent more than enough time out in the cold today and looked forward to a nice bowl of hot soup for dinner before she crashed for the day.

CHAPTER 14

Ghost emerged from the bathroom after his shower to find his room empty. Good. He'd hoped it was still a little early for Malice to be up to his usual shit. Ghost was able to get dressed and have his first cup of coffee in peace.

He had just poured his second cup, the TV on but muted as he watched the closed captioning and tickers across the bottom of the screen to find out what was going on in the world at large but not disturb the peace he was enjoying, when the door between his room and Malice's swept open.

Ghost didn't say anything, just turned to watch Malice step quietly into the room. Malice quietly closed the door then turned to find Ghost watching him.

"Damn. I was hoping you were either still asleep or in the shower again." Getting caught didn't dim the grin on his old partner's face.

Ghost rolled his eyes and watched as Malice went to the thermos sitting next to the coffee pot and helped himself to a cup, taking the last of the coffee. Then he went to the chair in the corner and sat, as if it was his own room.

"Why are you like this?" Ghost watched him a moment before turning back to the TV.

"Come on, admit it, you love me just the way I am."

"I don't know if I'd go that far," Ghost muttered as he checked the time. 7:28. "You heard anything from the dealership yet?"

"Nope and I probably won't for at least an hour, maybe two. Most dealerships won't open until eight or nine. I didn't look at this one's hours. You ready to go get something to eat?"

Ghost scrubbed a hand over his face. It was too early to start this shit, but he didn't have a choice.

"You want to go next door or somewhere else?" He'd hoped to drink at least another cup of coffee before Malice came in. There was no point in complaining about it and if he let his partner know how much the visits annoyed him, he would get up earlier tomorrow and be there when Ghost woke up.

"Have you looked outside yet? It dumped on us last night. The road looks pretty clean, but I'd rather let the sun shine on it for a bit before we go anywhere. Especially if we're going to Bismarck. I don't know how much of the interstate they kept plowed last night. Best give them a chance to get that done before we leave."

"Well, since it looks like it will be at least an hour till we hear about the truck, we might as well go eat. Let me get my boots on and we can walk over." He was going to need more coffee if Malice was going to continue to be so cheerful and annoying.

He wondered what he could do to the door to keep Malice from coming and going as he pleased. All the secure your lock commercial's he'd ever seen on TV flashed through his mind, but he instantly dismissed them because they'd been trying to sell something. Surely, he could find a way without having to order some device.

Ghost finished pulling on his boots, stood and shoved his phone into his pocket before grabbing his coat.

"Come on, I'm out of coffee."

Ghost didn't wait for Malice to stand before opening the door and stepping out into the biting wind. The snow might have stopped falling, but it hadn't warmed up any. A glance up told him the clouds from the day before were gone, and along with them the warmth they'd kept closer to the ground. He waited for Malice to join him then closed his door, keeping the warmth inside. He'd appreciate coming back to that later.

"There's no point in standing out in this cold." Ghost turned and started for the restaurant on the lot next to the motel.

"We could take the truck," Malice suggested.

"We'll be there before the truck would warm up. No point. You need to get used to working and walking in the cold. You saw the ranch before we left. Most of the work we do is outside."

"But you don't walk everywhere. I saw snow machines."

"We do use snow machines, and four-wheelers and dirt bikes when there's no snow, but not for everything. There's a lot of walking too."

"I don't mind walking. I'm just not fond of the cold." Malice rubbed his hands up and down his upper arms then folded his arms tight as they made their way across the still snow covered parking lot.

Ghost turned and stared at Malice a moment as they kept moving.

"How long did you say you'd been in Billings?"

"A few weeks," Malice said with a shrug. "I'd been working construction and moving with the work then the weather got too bad, and construction stopped."

"You need a better coat and gloves. It's cold out here but you shouldn't be that cold if you've got good outerwear. Not yet. We'll look at picking something up for you when we're in Bismarck."

"You act like we've already made the deal on the truck. They may not accept your offer."

"I know. But it's not a question of if we make the deal, unless the truck is already sold. It's a matter of how good of deal we can make. Either way, we'll make a deal, either on that truck or another. We need the extra vehicle for concealment on this job, and I can use it off this assignment too." They reached the little restaurant, Ghost opened the door and let Malice enter first, then stepped inside. Malice held the inner door open for him then followed him inside.

⚜

By the time they'd finished a surprisingly good breakfast and Ghost had drank several more cups of coffee, the dealership had reached out to Malice. They had gone back and forth a couple times, Malice said he felt like they'd come to an agreement. So far, Ghost was okay with the terms they'd hammered out.

While they had been exchanging emails and Ghost drank coffee, Ghost watched as the snowplow had cleared the street. He could only hope they'd gotten the interstate done or at least the section between Dickenson and Bismarck. Still, he wanted to give them a little more time to make sure there weren't any big snarls in traffic, because he knew as soon as the road was cleared the big rigs would head out. He wanted to give them a little time to move on before they got out on the highway.

"How much did you get them to come down from the asking price?"

"We settled at a little under six thousand under the asking price. I think that's better than you're going to find anywhere else."

Ghost nodded. He agreed. It was more than what he'd been after so he would take it. He pulled out his own phone and looked up where the nearest branch of his bank was located.

"Send the salesman another message, ask the exact amount and who to make the cashier's check out to." If he could get that, he'd get the check here in town before making the drive. That would make it closer to when he was wanting to leave town.

After Malice sent the message, Ghost asked for the ticket, paid for their meals and they went back to the motel. There was no point going to the bank until he knew how much to have the check made for. And once the check was made, the dealership couldn't add crap on to jack the price up. That alone was worth the hassle of dealing with the bank when buying a vehicle.

CHAPTER 15

Robyn had been relieved to find no new snow had fallen while she'd slept. At least she wouldn't have to dig her car out before work. And that was a good thing because for some reason her alarm hadn't gone off, or if it had it didn't wake her, and she'd had to hurry getting ready. She was headed to work now, wishing she'd had time for more than a single cup of coffee.

Oh, well, I'll get another cup at work. Let's face reality, she told herself, *I'll have several more than one more during my shift.*

She made the last turn before turning into the convenience store and glanced at the clock. *Almost. If the lights are with me, I might just make it on time.* As she approached the store, Robyn kept glancing at the clock, hoping she made it on time. She hated being late. She'd rather be thirty minutes early than a single minute late.

Almost there, another half a block to go.

Oh shit. There is someone walking across the road.

Fuck, fuck, fuck, fuck. Do I have time to stop?

There would be ice on the road.

Robyn pumped the breaks. *The last thing I need to do is lock my brakes or hit a patch of black ice and slide into the dark figure making their way across the road.* Her heart thundered in her ears.

Please, please, please, don't let me hit him.

It seemed like she was already on top of him when she felt the breaks catch, the car slowed. It was still going too fast, but she'd slowed enough that she could turn the wheel without risking flipping the car and hitting him with the side instead of the front of the car.

Holding her breath, she turned the wheel, praying she didn't hit a patch of ice, and the car did what she told it to.

Luck was on her side. The car swerved, shuddered then did what she wanted. The man saw her just as she was sure she wasn't going to hit him. The car was still moving a little fast as she pulled into the parking lot of her work. She pulled into the parking space, shifted into park, and killed the engine, then sat in the driver's seat shaking and trying to catch her breath.

She didn't know how long she'd been sitting there when a knock sounded on the window beside her. She jumped, and turned to find the man who had been coming into the shop each night. The one she'd been looking forward to seeing, the one she kept finding herself thinking about.

Oh God. Did he see that? Even worse, was he the one I almost hit? Her heart thundered in her chest. She couldn't seem to catch her breath.

She wanted to huddle in the car and hide but it was too late for that. She had to face him. Instead of rolling down the window she opened the door. He stepped back to let the door swing open then moved forward.

"Are you okay?" the man she'd been mooning over for the last few days asked.

Robyn opened her mouth to ask if she'd hit him, but his question had her stopping without saying anything. She blinked then tried again. "I'm fine. I didn't hit you, did I?"

"No. What happened? Did you hit a patch of ice?"

Robyn shook her head. "I was running late and trying to get here on time. I'm so, so sorry." She stood but nearly as soon as she reached her feet, her knees gave way and she started to go down. Desperate not to land on her ass in front of the guy who made heat pool in her nether regions, she reached for the car door, but an arm went around her waist, and he stepped closer.

"Are you sure you're all right?" He sounded concerned as his words breathed across the shell of one ear. "You didn't step on ice, did you?"

Robyn shifted her feet then took a deep breath and pushed herself to her feet again, this time it seemed like her knees held.

"I think I'm good now, thank you," she said.

His grip around her waist eased slowly, as if making sure she wasn't going to fall again before he released her and stepped back. "Are you sure you're okay?"

Robyn nodded. "Just a little shaken up. I'm good. Again. I'm so sorry. I'm also mortified I almost hit you."

"You didn't, so we're all good." He waved one hand in dismissal.

"Still. I'd like to try to make it up to you. How about I treat you to breakfast at my favorite diner? Show you one of the best parts of

Dickenson?" As soon as the words were out of her mouth, she realized how they sounded. Her face heated and she could only hope he didn't take it the way she hadn't meant it. Well… on the other hand, it might be fun if she took him for a spin. Her face grew even hotter, if that was possible.

"Breakfast?" He paused, the deep rumble of his voice sending heat to pool low in her belly. "I'd like that. What time does your shift end?"

She told him, then realized she'd been standing here for several minutes talking to him. There was no way she wasn't late. She apologized again, then let him know she had to get inside, as she was running late, then hurried inside.

In the door, she hurried past Harry and into the back to clock in and put her things away. Maybe she wouldn't need so much coffee to get through the shift after all.

CHAPTER 16

Ghost couldn't believe his luck. He had been lost in his thoughts when he'd spotted the car sliding toward him. He'd already been moving to try and get out of the way when the driver had managed to turn it into the parking lot.

It wasn't until he'd stopped to check on the driver, making sure they were all right, that he'd realized it was the girl he'd been talking to each night, the one who worked here. The one he'd been hoping to see.

He hadn't been planning to see her coming straight at him on the road.

She opened the car door.

"Are you okay?" he asked. Her face was so pale he thought she might be hurt, or maybe sick. Was it something more than just the roads that had caused the near accident?

She opened her mouth, then closed it. After a moment she tried again. "I'm fine. I didn't hit you, did I?"

"No. What happened? Did you hit a patch of ice?"

The woman shook her head. "I was running late and trying to get here on time. I'm so, so sorry." She tried to stand but before she could make it all the way to her feet, she fell.

Ghost had been trying to keep his distance, he didn't want to scare her by getting too close, but when she fell, he followed his instincts, stepped closer and caught her with an arm around her waist.

"Are you sure you're all right?" He tilted his head and tried to look at her face. He hoped he hadn't scared her when he caught her. "You didn't step on ice, did you?"

He felt her take a deep breath then try to stand again. This time it went better.

"I think I'm good now, thank you," she said.

Ghost eased his grip around her waist slowly, trying to be sure she wasn't going to fall again, then released her and stepped back. "Are you sure you're okay?"

She nodded. "Just a little shaken up. I'm good. Again. I'm so sorry. I'm also mortified I almost hit you."

"You didn't so we're all good." He quickly dismissed her embarrassment. They were both safe, that's what mattered.

"Still. I'd like to try to make it up to you. How about I treat you to breakfast at my favorite diner? Show you one of the best parts of Dickenson?" She blushed as soon as she'd finished speaking.

Ghost assumed her innuendo had been unintentional. He didn't want to embarrass her further by mentioning it, so he ignored it.

"Breakfast?" Ghost tilted his head and watched her a moment. He'd love a chance to sit and talk to her for more than a minute or two but hated that she was only asking as an apology. "I'd like that. What time does your shift end?" There was no way he was going to let her buy him breakfast, but he'd wait until it was time to pick up the tab to tell her that.

"Five-thirty, but I can wait until later if that's better for you. Oh, crap I'm so late. I've got to get inside. I can talk to you in there in a few minutes." She closed the car door as she turned and hurried inside, leaving him standing, watching her go.

Ghost didn't know how long he stood there, watching where she'd disappeared through the door. It wasn't until another car pulled into the station that he realized he should go in and get what he was after.

This trip he was after a sixpack of beer. He hadn't even brought his thermos. He'd planned to come in later for that.

Still, he wanted to talk to her more, maybe get her number, but at least find out her name. Yeah, he needed to know her name.

Ghost followed her into the store to at least get her name, and hopefully her number. The beer wouldn't hurt either.

***

"That took a long time to just walk across the road and get beer," Malice said as Ghost let himself into his room.

"Yeah, well, it was more complicated than just getting beer." He debated whether or not to tell his partner about nearly getting hit but decided to go ahead and tell him. "I almost got hit crossing the road."

"Shit. Was it the guys we've been tracking?"

Ghost shook his head. "No. It was an accident."

"Are you sure? It could be someone tied to this group."

"No. It was the girl who works at the station. She was so shaken up and scared from the whole thing, I have no doubt she didn't do it on purpose."

Malice watched him, as if trying to read him. "But you forgot the beer."

"I didn't forget. They don't have any. Must be something to do with the liquor laws here. When I asked, they said I can get it at a grocery store, drug store, liquor store and some convenience stores sell it, but they'd decided it was just too much hassle, so they don't carry alcohol."

"Bummer, I was looking forward to that."

"You're welcome to take one of the trucks and find some if you want, but I've had enough for now. I'll go back over later and fill up my coffee, but I'm going to relax for a bit before it's time to do that." He didn't say he was waiting until late to do that so he could go talk to Robyn more. He wanted more of a chance to talk to her with no one around. Yes, he'd have that chance in the morning, but in a restaurant, there would be people around.

That's when it hit him. She was usually on her phone when he walked in. And he'd gotten her number when she'd given him her name. He didn't have to wait until he went in later. He could text her now. If she was busy, that was fine. She'd find the message when she wasn't busy.

He kicked off his boots and shed his outer layer, so he could get comfortable then stretched out on the bed and turned on the tv. After turning it to something for background noise, and to keep Malice from realizing he was doing anything out of the ordinary, he pulled out his phone. He usually listened to whatever was on TV while reading news and researching different things, so there wasn't anything out of the ordinary in him being on his phone.

Ghost: Hi Robyn, it's Ghost. You gave me your number a little bit ago. I wanted to make sure you have mine.

He hit send then flipped over to read the headlines and find some thing to keep his mind busy until she replied. If she replied.

CHAPTER 17

Robyn felt her phone buzz in her pocket and assumed from the single vibration that it was a message of some kind but didn't pull it out because she was busy. There was a line of a half dozen people waiting to check out and once that was done, she had some chores to finish before she had time to kill.

She would see what the message was when she had time, it was probably some last-minute reminder from Harry anyway.

It wasn't until nearly an hour later she finally had a chance to sit down and rest for a couple of minutes. She dragged the stool closer to the register so she could use it if someone came in, then pulled out her phone and sat.

That's when she saw the message from Ghost. What kind of name was Ghost anyway? She didn't bother to try to stop the smile that crept across her face as she thought about the way he'd followed her inside and checked on her again before asking for her number. He'd been really sweet, and she hadn't worried a bit about giving it to him, which she had with some of the men she'd dated in the past.

Robyn: Hey. Glad you thought to give it to me. So, what time you want to go to breakfast?

She hit send, then closed her eyes and forced the butterflies fluttering in her stomach to calm down. It had been a long time since he'd sent her the message, it would likely be a while before he saw hers. She navigated to the game she'd been playing, but before it had time to load, her phone vibrated in her hand, and a message from Ghost flashed across the top of her screen.

Ghost: I'm good with 0530 when you get off. Want me to swing by and pick you up?

She started to tell him no, she could take him, but after almost hitting him this afternoon, why would he want to get in a car with her driving? She could meet him there, but why not ride with him? The idea of sitting beside him in a vehicle sent tendrils of heat through her belly.

Robyn: Sure. That way I can give you directions on how to get there.

She thought that was the end of it, so she went back to her game, but again, it didn't have time to load before another message buzzed in.

Ghost: I can't wait to see you, but until then we can get to know each other a little. Are you from Dickenson?

Heat washed through her. Starting at her toes and working its way up her body all the way through the top of her head then back down again until it pooled low in her tummy. She didn't know why, but that he was interested in her made her feel all hot and bothered.

Robyn: I am. Spent most of my life here. I left for a while but came back. Didn't have anywhere else I wanted to be at the time.

This time she didn't bother to leave the messaging app. She just waited as the icons danced telling her he was typing a message then it came through.

Ghost: Is there anything holding you here, or you just didn't have anywhere else you wanted to be?

Robyn thought about that for a moment. She'd always liked to travel, but this had been home. She'd left a few times, gone to visit Mom in Texas, but she liked it at home too.

Robyn: This is home. There was never anything to keep me away for long.

She shoved her phone in her pocket and went about getting a couple more of the cleanup chores she had to do overnight done. It kept her from staring at the screen while she waited for him to reply. When her phone buzzed, she finished the job, and put away all her supplies before pulling her phone out and seeing what he had to say.

Ghost: What would it take to get you to think of somewhere else as home?

She went back behind the counter and sat down to type up her answer.

Robyn: I believe home is more the people in your life than a place. It would take someone becoming more important to me than the people here.

The tones indicating a customer chimed as she was typing up her reply. She looked up and welcomed them, then finished her message and hit send while they shopped. Once she sent the message, she looked up to find the older woman who had come in earlier approaching the counter, several items in her hands. Robyn shoved her phone back in her pocket and smiled at the other woman.

"Did you find everything okay?"

"I did, thanks. Do you know if we're supposed to get more storms in the next couple days?"

"I'm sorry. I haven't heard and I really don't stay on top of the weather. I probably should since so many people stop in and ask." Robyn gave the woman a wry smile as she finished ringing up the purchases then gave her the total. While they were waiting for her card to clear, Robyn's phone buzzed in her pocket. She ignored it and finished bagging up the woman's items, then bid her good night and waited until the door swung closed behind her before pulling out her phone to see what Ghost had sent.

Ghost: So, for the right person, you might be willing to leave Dickenson?

Robyn frowned at her screen, was he hoping to maybe that right person? Why else would he ask something like this?

Robyn: For the right person, I'd go anywhere.

She thought for a moment. What was the most unpleasant place she could think of? Where might she be willing to go to be with the right person?

After a moment she thought better of sending something like that. She had no clue where he was from, and what if she picked where he lived as an unpleasant place? What could she send that would be innocuous? After a moment she settled on something.

Robyn: But I think I'm safe for a while since I'm not dating anyone anyway.

Was that too obvious? She hoped not. Robyn didn't know why just the thought of him did things to her body. She hadn't even seen his entire face. He always had his hat pulled down, so his eyebrows were almost lost in the knit fabric. She didn't even know what color his hair was. She'd barely even learned his name.

The phone buzzed in her hand making her realize she'd been staring off into space. It seemed like her heart skipped a beat as she turned the screen back on to see what he'd said.

Ghost: That's good news for me. On both fronts.

Robyn stared at her screen, mouth hanging open. He was hitting on her. But why? Did he have a thing for near death experiences and the cause of them? She hoped not because she'd really like to get to know him better. Maybe figure out why he set off her libido every time he took a breath in her vicinity. She didn't know how to respond. What could she say? She'd like to get to know him better?

Robin didn't know how long she sat there, staring at her phone, and trying to decide what to say when the buzzer on the door went off, alerting her to a customer.

"Welcome," she said as she lifted her head and spotted Ghost walking in, a smile on his face as he carried his thermos to the coffee pot and began filling it and fixing himself an extra cup, just as he had every evening since he'd brought the thermos. Had it only been a couple days?

He did his usual turn through the candy aisle, then came up to the counter and grinned at her again.

"Did I render you speechless?"

She shook her head then blinked. Robyn knew she was acting like an idiot, but he had been the last person she'd been expecting to see at that moment.

"No. I just had to make my brain shift gears. I have so many questions, but some of them are better face to face and I wanted to save those for tomorrow when we're sitting down, and I can watch your reactions. But I do have one question since you're here."

"What's that?"

"Why Ghost?"

He chuckled. "It's my call sign."

"Call sign?"

"Kind of like a nickname, it started as a name used on the radio, shorter than last names usually, but it my case it was more unique."

"Radio? Are you a cop?"

He grinned again and shook his head. "Not a cop, and you're the only one to suggest that ever. I was in the marines."

"Oh. That makes more sense. But can I ask your real name?"

"You can ask… and I might even tell you. But no one has called me that in so long I don't even react."

She rang up his purchases, smiling as she realized not only was he buying two containers of coffee each night, he was getting two packages of candy.

"Are you the one with the sweet tooth or are you sharing with someone else?"

His smile grew until the sides of his eyes crinkled a bit, "My teammate keeps trying to talk me out of some, but I won't share." He lifted one shoulder in a half shrug. "If I'm willing to trek out in the cold to feed my sweet tooth, then he can do the same. Besides, he could use getting out and getting a little exercise. It will give him something to do besides irritate me."

Robyn couldn't help smiling at Ghost's grumpy tone. Something about it was endearing.

"Have a good night. I guess I'll see you in the morning."

"I'll see you then." His smile turned from wry to genuine. "I'll pick you up at 5:30."

"I can walk over there if that would be easier."

Ghost shook his head. "I don't like the idea of you walking, even that short distance, in the dark. Too much can happen in the dark."

She started to protest that she walked in the dark all the time here, but somehow knew that wouldn't help. Instead, she smiled. "Okay, then I'll be ready and waiting here."

"Great, see you then." He stuffed the candy in his pockets, picked up his coffee and left.

CHAPTER 18

Ghost was up, showered, and ready to go by 0500, when he looked out the window to make sure he didn't need to clean off the truck. Then he sat drinking coffee and waiting until 0520 so he wouldn't look like a stalker by showing up for her a half hour early.

He wrote a note for Malice and put it on the table where the other man had made a habit of sitting when he snuck into Ghost's room. The note told him he'd gone out for breakfast, and that the other man was welcome to do the same, but please swing by wherever the locater said their subject was, to make sure it was still on the truck. They'd talk more when Ghost returned. He spent the rest of the wait hoping Malice wouldn't decide to try to sneak in earlier and catch him asleep. Then he'd have to answer a million questions and tell his partner why he wasn't welcome to join him for breakfast and he'd rather not have to do that, not yet.

Finally, the clock changed over, and he felt like it wasn't too early to leave. He finished putting on all his outer wear, grabbed his keys, coffee cup and the card that was his room key and slipped outside, still being as quiet as he could. It wasn't until he'd pulled out of the parking lot without either his door or Malice's opening that he breathed a sigh of relief.

It only took a moment or two to get across the road to the convenience store and park beside Robyn's car. He didn't go inside or kill the engine, just waited for her to come out.

By the time she emerged from the building, gloves on and scarf wrapped tight around her neck, the cab of the truck was nice and warm. Ghost hit the button on his door that unlocked the passenger's side, then waited while she climbed up inside.

"How was your shift?" he asked once she was seated inside and had the door closed.

"Good, I guess." She shrugged then buckled her seat belt.

Ghost watched her for a moment, trying to read her face, but he didn't know her well enough to know what small changes in her face meant, at least not yet. He had hopes he would soon though.

"I'm glad. Now tell me where we're going." He backed out of the space and followed her directions out onto the street and through the light.

"Are you usually up this early?" she asked after telling him where to turn.

"Depends on what I'm doing. I have been recently because I've been working on a ranch, and we get up early to take care of the cattle and get stuff done. I like to get up before the rest of the hands, so I get some time to myself before they're up and chattering non-stop." He kept an eye on the road, watching for other cars and other hazards, like patches of ice.

"Why did you leave?"

"I didn't really. I'm still working for the ranch, but they've got me up here on some business." He turned and flashed her a quick smile before taking the next turn as she'd instructed.

"Oh? How long will you be in town?"

"Not sure. It depends on how long it takes to get our business concluded. But I find myself hoping it takes longer and longer each day."

"Why is that?"

A glance and the glow of the streetlights that gave him enough light to see her face, told him she had a crease between her brows as she watched him in confusion.

He couldn't stop himself before the wry smile lifted one corner of his mouth. "I found this girl, and I'm not sure what, but something about her makes me want to get to know her better. The only way I can do that is with time, so I need more time in Dickenson." He glanced in her direction and attempted to judge her reaction, but between the dim light and not knowing her well enough, he didn't know if she understood she was who he was talking about.

CHAPTER 19

Who was the girl he wanted to get to know better? Robyn couldn't help but wonder. She wanted it to be her, but even after the texting they'd done last night, she couldn't begin to hope. They barely knew each other. How could it be her?

"I hope you can be around long enough to know her as well as you like." There, that was safe. She hadn't let it show how much she wished it was her he wanted to know, but had wished him well either way.

She gave Ghost the last of the directions and waited while he pulled into the lot and parked. He didn't open the door right away, instead he twisted in his seat as much as he could until he almost faced her.

"Robyn?"

"Yeah?" She watched his face in the pale glow from the street lights, noticing how it left his eyes mostly in shadow, but she could see the lower half of his face almost perfectly.

"I think you couldn't tell, which is why I'm saying it like this now." He paused.

She frowned, not sure what he was going to say.

"Robyn, you are the girl I want to get to know."

Her face heated. the cab of the truck had started to cool since he'd killed the engine moments before, but it wasn't yet cold enough that her face should feel like it was flaming, but here she was.

"Oh." She looked down at her hands, not sure what to say next. "I'm glad it's me. I wanted it to be me, but was afraid to hope." She paused and looked back up to meet his gaze. "I want to get to know you better too."

A grin spread across his face and Robyn couldn't help but mirror it. It made her heart beat faster.

"Come on, let's go eat. I can't wait to taste your favorite breakfast joint in town." He turned away and opened the door, breaking the spell that seemed to hold her hostage staring at him. She opened her door, climbed down from the lifted pickup, and went inside with him.

Once they were seated and had menus, Ghost laid his on the table and scanned it, then without looking up, spoke.

"What do you like here?"

Robyn glanced down at the menu then back up to Ghost who was watching her now.

"Everything I've tried is good. I'm particularly fond of the country fried steak and eggs, and the biscuits and gravy." She looked down at the table again. "But I guess if you're not much on gravy, neither would be very appealing." Robyn looked back at him in time to find Ghost staring down at his menu again.

"I'm good with gravy. I know some people don't like it, but I do. Do they use ground beef or sausage in the biscuits and gravy here?"

"Beef. I've had some with sausage and most of the time it's good, but once in a while you'll find where they used an odd sausage and that throws the whole thing off."

He nodded without saying anything for a few minutes. When the waitress came back for their orders, Robyn gave hers first, opting for the country fried steak and eggs, and couldn't help her surprise when he ordered the biscuits and gravy, as well as eggs and bacon, though it wasn't the eggs that surprised her. She'd thought from his reaction that he wasn't into beef in his gravy. Hmm.

Once the waitress had left, Ghost sat back in his seat and watched her a moment before speaking.

"Do you like working nights?"

"I do. It's quiet. I see a lot of the same people most nights, though there are people passing through and different things happen, but I have a lot of time to myself, and I like that."

"Do you worry about being the only one there all night?"

Robyn shook her head. "My dad does, and Mom never stops worrying and trying to tell me how to live my life. But I have a lot of police officers who stop in through the night to check on me. I'm friends with some of them, and I'm not worried."

Something about her response seemed to be right because his friendly smile grew into a grin. "I'm going to guess that when the weather isn't miserable you walk back and forth, even in the dark, don't you?"

Her face heated again. "Maybe."

"And from your reaction, you don't tell the people who worry about you the most that you do, because then they'll worry more, and maybe nag you about it more."

"Maybe." She watched out the window beside their table because she didn't want to let him read her face as easily as he seemed to be doing. "Tell me more about you? Where is the ranch you work at?"

"Wyoming. Near Gillette."

"Wow, that's a way from here. What brought you all the way to North Dakota?"

Ghost tilted his head back and looked at the ceiling a moment, she wasn't sure if he was trying to decide whether to answer her or how much he could share.

"We had a couple of guys hanging around the entrance to the ranch. They would wait for my boss's wife or the foreman's girlfriend to leave, then follow them and harass them wherever they were when not on the ranch. They followed the foreman's girlfriend and confronted her one day, threatened her. They were generally harassing the women."

Robyn's heart thundered in her chest. She'd been on the receiving end of someone following her around and it was terrifying. She hated that these women she didn't know had gone through that.

"That sucks. Did you get them to stop?"

Ghost shook his head. "We tried. We cornered them, confronted them, tried to scare them off, but they kept at it. We're fed up with this and need to know why. I thought they might go back wherever they came from for the holidays, so I started watching them myself. When they left the area, we followed."

She wondered why they'd stopped in Dickenson then. Robyn tilted her head and watched him, waiting for him to continue. It only took her a few second to realize what had happened.

"They stopped here. You're still watching them."

Ghost nodded. "We are."

"We?"

"I mentioned that I have a buddy here with me, didn't I?

She frowned and tried to remember.

"You didn't say buddy, but you did say you're here with a teammate. You said he keeps trying to talk you out of your candy when you got your coffee last night."

"That's right, I did. Anyway, he's the other half of the 'we'. We're working on figuring out who they are." He tilted his head to one side and looked at her a moment. "You know this area and who's in it. Do you know anything about any local motorcycle clubs?"

"There is one. I don't know anyone in it, but you see them rumbling around on their bikes often enough when there's not snow everywhere."

"Do you happen to remember what they call themselves?"

She started to say of course she did but when she tried to call the name of the club to mind, she drew a blank.

"I know the club, but I can't think of the name. Give me a few minutes and it will come to me."

"No problem. Aside from the name, do you know anything about them? Are they troublemakers? Active in the community? That kind of thing?"

"You mean like fundraisers, Toys for Tots, that kind of thing?"

"Exactly."

"No. Not that I am aware of, and I try to donate to toy collections when I can, so I would have noticed that. A lot of groups doing fundraising will come into the store and ask to put out a bin or post a flyer, and I haven't seen those either so it's a safe bet to say they're neither."

Ghost nodded, and it looked like he was about to say something when the name of the motorcycle club popped into her head.

"Kings of Destruction. That's what those patches on their vests say."

"Kings of Destruction. You're sure?" He pulled out his phone then looked at her before doing anything else.

"I am. I remember thinking it was a dumb name, Kings part I kind of get, most of them that I've encountered act like they're above the rest of the town, but destruction? Why would you brag about something like that?"

"Give me just a sec. I'm sending a message to a techie friend of mine to do some research on the Kings of Destruction and see what he can find." He typed out a message, hit send and put his phone back in his pocket. "Since we're on the subject, how do you feel about motorcycles?"

She lifted one shoulder in a half shrug.

"I've never thought much about them."

"Are you against them? Have you ever been on one?"

Robyn watched him a moment, tilting her head to one side. "I've never been on one, but I've got nothing against them." She wondered why he would ask something like this.

"If the weather were better, and I had mine up here, I'd offer to take you for a ride, but only a fool is going to take a bike out in this ice. Driving is dangerous enough in a car or truck."

A thrill raced through Robyn at the idea of climbing on the back of a motorcycle behind Ghost. Wrapping her arms around him and trusting him to keep her safe as they sped along on two wheels.

"I think I'd like that. Is your bike in Gillette?"

"Yeah. I rode it up from Tucson in the fall, not realizing I wouldn't want to use it for months on end. Then I regretted not having my truck instead."

"Is this where I say but you're driving a truck?" She gave him what she hoped was a flirtatious smile.

"That's a ranch truck, but I did buy a truck recently, so I won't be stuck driving my employer's vehicles if I want to go somewhere personal."

Robyn wondered for a moment where he might want to go, then realized this is a long way to take a company truck if he wasn't on work business. Was he wanting to come back up to see her?

The waitress came with their food, saving her from having to respond right away.

CHAPTER 20

Ghost thought things had gone well as they headed back out to the truck. After eating they'd sat talking and drinking coffee for nearly an hour before she'd told him she needed to get home and get a few things done before bed. Now he was taking her back to her car, then he'd go back to the motel and find out what Gizmo had found out about the Kings of Destruction.

"I think I can get us back to the station, but you'll need to correct me if I miss a turn or go the wrong way," he said as he started the truck.

"Not a problem. I had a really good time this morning, but this was supposed to be my apologizing to you for nearly running you down. You were not supposed to pay for our meals."

"I had a good time too. I've been trying to figure out how to ask you out without coming across like some kind of creeper, so there was no way I was going to let you pay for it." He shot her a grin then turned back to the road. The sun had come up and it was easier to see where they were going, as well as to see her face on those quick glances he took her way. "Along that line, I'd like to see you again."

She was quiet long enough he glanced her way and found her watching him, an intrigued look on her face.

"I'd like that too," she said after what seemed like an eon but was probably under a minute. "What are you doing tomorrow?"

"That's the catch, I'm not sure yet. I need to go back to my room, find out if my contact has found anything on the Kings of Destruction, then see if we can come up with a plan on how to figure out why they're harassing the women around the ranch and how to get it to stop. I don't know what tomorrow looks like or how long I might be in town."

"Let's just worry about one day at a time. When you figure out what you're doing tomorrow, you have my number. Give me a call or a text and we'll see what we can plan."

"I'll do that. What time do you usually wake up? I know how hard it is to get enough sleep when you work nights, and I don't want to wake you on accident."

She gave him her schedule as he pulled the pickup into the space beside her car at the convenience store, and put it in park. Ghost turned to wish her a good day, and that she rest well, but Robyn was already up on one knee in the seat, stretching across the folded middle seat that acted as a console. She laid one hand along side his face, holding his face where she wanted it as she moved in and kissed him.

Ghost was so surprised that he didn't respond for probably three full seconds, then a groan tore itself from his throat as he parted his lips so she could taste him, and he could explore her mouth.

The sweet tang of the tea she'd had with her breakfast burst across his senses. He was barely aware of lifting his own hand until he felt Robyn's hair tangle in his fingers. His entire body responded. His eyes drifted closed, he leaned in, and his cock hardened in his jeans, making him ache for more.

Ghost lost all track of time, and the rest of the world ceased to matter as long as Robyn was here, not quite in his arms but close enough. He could have kissed her for hours. Well, he would like it to go farther than that, but he'd take kissing if that was all he could get.

When she pulled away, he wanted to growl and pull her back, he wanted to tug her on to his lap and let her see how snug his jeans had become. But he let her go.

"I've got to go." Her words were little more than a breath across his skin.

"That's one hell of a way to make sure I reach out to you tonight, sunshine."

"Sunshine?" A crease appeared between her brows.

"You are something special, and you smell like springtime. You're a bright spot of sunshine in this cold frozen place." He reached up to run the edge of his thumb along her jaw. "Go, get some rest. I'll reach out tonight to let you know what's up and when we can get together again. I want another one of those kisses." She leaned close again and Ghost couldn't resist another quick taste of her lips, but he pulled back this time instead of waiting for her. "Go, before I lose my grip on my control and pull you over here into my lap. Then it will be a long time before we get out of here. And

I'm sure you don't want to get caught making out in the parking lot at work."

He was glad to see the heat in her eyes nearly matched his, but the heat dimmed a little when he reminded her where they were.

"You're right. I don't. I'll hear from you tonight though?"

"I promise. I don't know if it will be call or text, but I'll be in touch tonight. Sleep well."

She gave him one last smile before sliding from the seat of the truck. He watched as she got into her car and pulled out of the lot before backing out and making his way over to the motel.

"So, you found you some piece of ass all the way up here?" Malice's voice asked as soon as Ghost stepped into the room.

Ghost rolled his eyes, but let the comment go. This time.

"I went to breakfast with a nice girl who wanted to apologize for nearly running me down. At the same time, I found some valuable information about the asshats we followed up here. Have you been as productive?"

Malice opened his mouth, to come back with a smart ass remark, Ghost was sure, then closed it without saying anything. He visibly swallowed, and it looked painful, then spoke.

"What did you learn?"

"The name of the local MC. I sent it to Gizmo a couple hours ago. I'm getting ready to call and see if he's found out anything. Or if he's even had a chance to start looking."

"Gizmo?"

"I fell so easy into our old dynamic I sometimes forget you're new the club. Gizmo is our tech sergeant in Tucson. He's a wiz with computers and research."

"Ah."

"You want to listen in and see what we can find out?"

"You're up for that?" Malice lifted both brows.

"Sure. Let me get comfortable then I'll call." He kicked off his boots and stripped out of his jacket before grabbing the notebook he'd picked up when they'd gone shopping. Sometimes putting pen to paper helped him think and connect things to each other. He sat on the edge of the bed, put the notebook on the table and dialed the phone, hitting speaker before setting it on the table beside the notebook while it still rang.

"Yo, how are things in the frigid tundra?" Gizmo's familiar voice came across the line when he picked up.

"Cold, but you know I'm not in the tundra. There are trees, but not that many."

"More than here."

"That's true. Did you get the name I texted you earlier?"

"Kings of Destruction? I did, but I'm busy with something going on here and don't have time to do the research. I handed it off to Krissi a little over an hour ago."

"So, I need to call her."

"You will. I don't know how much she'll have yet, but it can't hurt to check."

"I don't have her number."

"I'll text it to you. Anything else I can help you with?"

"Not that I can think of. I'll be in touch if the is anything."

"You know where to find me. And it's not where I'd freeze my balls off like you."

"I didn't know you were so interested in my balls. I don't swing that way, bro, but I will tell you my balls are happy right where they are."

CHAPTER 21

Robyn drove home almost on autopilot. Her mind wasn't on the road or the traffic around her, but instead back in the cab of that pickup with Ghost. Heat pooled in her belly as she remembered the way his hand felt buried in her hair. His taste and the soft scrape of his beard against her skin.

After pulling into her driveway, she waved at Mrs. Morgan who opened her curtain as if she was waiting for someone, then hurried inside. As much as she loved the rare sunshine this time of year, the temperature seemed to drop, and she didn't want to fuss with tightening her scarf for the trip inside.

Once she stepped into the house and closed the door, she reminded herself to thank Dad again for talking her into the programmable thermostat, so the place was nice and toasty, or as toasty as she ever set it, when she'd come in. Now she didn't have to wait for it to warm up.

Stripping out of her outer later, she hung her things up next to the door then padded through the house to get ready for bed. It had been a great morning, and she'd enjoyed the time with Ghost, but now putting off bedtime was coming back to haunt her. Her whole body ached, and she wished she'd had the nerve to invite him home with her. At least then he'd be here and the warmth of him next to her would help ease some of the exhausted ache.

Plus, she wouldn't have to imagine how he'd be in bed. Now, as she changed into her night gown, brushed out her hair, washed her face and brushed her teeth, she wondered what a night with him would be like and when, or if, she would build up the nerve to invite him home with her. Or maybe he would invite her to his motel room.

If he did, would she go?

Who was she kidding? Of course, she would go. But what she really wanted was him here, in her bed. But it would take more than a single meal before she was ready to trust him in her space.

She slid between the sheets, then made sure her alarm was set before reaching over her head and pulling her vibrator from the cabinet in the headboard where she kept a couple different models. It only took her a moment to find the right one by touch. She pulled it out and set it on the bed next to her while she got ready.

Robyn closed her eyes and let her mind drift back to Ghost. She remembered the feeling of his hand on her skin. The tug as he'd slid his hand into her hair. She called to mind the clean scent of his skin and the sweetened coffee he'd tasted of.

While she let images of Ghost run through her mind, Robyn let her hands roam over her skin. She caressed her breasts, pretending the hands on her weren't her own but his instead. It took her a moment to get into the swing of it, her fingers toyed with her nipples, rolling and pinching them until her body moved restlessly as it cried out for more. Still imagining it was Ghost and not her own hands, Robyn let one hand drift down her body and over her mound. Her fingers parted the slick folds between her thighs and circled the sensitive nub nestled near the front.

A moan escaped her lips.

Robyn reached for the toy she'd left beside her a few moments earlier, hit the power button and slid it between her thighs. The toy not only vibrated, but it gave a gentle sucking sensation when she lowered it to that oh-so sensitive spot. She pictured the hot look in Ghost's eyes after their kiss and imagined it was him looking up at her from between her thighs.

Between the images in her head and the sensations her toy gave, it only took a couple of minutes before Robyn's back arched, her head fell back against the pillow, and she didn't bother to hold back her cries of release.

After shutting off the toy, she laid there for several moments, waiting for her breathing to return to normal and the jelly feeling to leave her muscles. After cleaning up, she slid back beneath the sheets and drifted off to sleep. The only thing missing was the warmth of Ghost there beside her.

When her alarm went off, Robyn rolled over and picked up her phone, shut the alarm off and scrolled through the alerts she hadn't even heard while she'd slept.

A text from her mother, she'd reply to her later. An email reminding her she needed to get the oil changed in her car. Nothing of any real importance, but she lay in bed, letting it occupy her because she wasn't yet ready to get up. Getting up was sometimes harder than others. Most days she made it up with little problem but others, it took her ten or fifteen minutes to force herself upright and moving.

The phone was in her hand when it chimed with an incoming text. Her heart seemed to skip a beat when it flashed who the message was from and the first few words across the top of the screen. She stared unseeing at the screen for several seconds before realizing how foolish she was being and going to her messages so she could read the whole thing.

Ghost: Hey sunshine. You up yet? Missed talking to you today.

While she was thinking about how to reply, another message came in.

Ghost: Hope I didn't wake you. You've been on my mind all day and I just wanted to say good morning, or good evening, however you think of it.

Ghost: Maybe good waking up?

Robyn couldn't help the small laugh that his rapid-fire texting and running commentary caused.

Robyn: I'm awake. Missed you today too, but mostly before I slept. Could have used you then. I'm going to hop in the shower, I'll be back in a bit.

She threw the blankets back, hopped out of bed and left the phone on the sheets as she headed for the shower. She needed to get in so she could get out and see what Ghost had to say next.

CHAPTER 22

Ghost called Kristi, but it went to voicemail. Rather than leave a message with what he was after, something that could be hacked, he texted her.

Ghost: This is Ghost. I need to talk to you, please call when you can.

He knew there was something that would keep her from responding right away but he couldn't recall what it was off hand. Maybe it would come to him before she called back.

"Now what?" Malice asked.

"Now we check on the truck. Why don't you take the GPS and the new truck and do that? I'll wait here in case Krissi calls back. I don't want to risk hitting an area with no signal and miss her call."

"All right," Malice said with a nod. He stood.

Ghost scooted back until he wasn't just sitting on the edge of the bed, so Malice had room to get between him and the table, then he watched as his partner disappeared through the adjoining doors and closed them.

Ghost took a deep breath and tried to let go of the tension that had settled into his shoulders the moment Malice had called Robyn a piece of ass. He'd wanted to rip the other man's head off, but had managed to hold onto his temper, if only by the skin of his teeth, and keep the focus where he'd wanted it. Where he needed it.

On the Kings of Destruction.

He stood, taking his phone with him and googled the name Robyn had given him. There were a few mentions, but nothing having to do with Dickenson, or even North Dakota in general. There were a couple hits that mentioned Billings, Montana. Ghost dismissed those as being too far away to be the men he was looking for. If they were based out of Billings, why had they come here and spent several days here?

The new truck started outside, letting him know Malice was leaving. Something else occurred to him and he sent his partner a quick message.

Ghost: Swing by that warehouse too, if that's not where the GPS takes you. Watch it for a few minutes if you can. See if anything of interest happens and what you can see from the place.

With the message sent he stretched out on his bed and tried to think about the reason they were here. The men harassing the women at the ranch and why. In all likely hood, it had to do with the Demented Souls, or at least that was Ghost's suspicion now that he knew it was another club. Before following the asshats all the way up here, and finding out they're from a club, he'd suspected they'd been set on them by Levi Crawford.

Levi was a neighboring rancher in Gillette, and just as importantly in Ghost's mind, Tuck's teenage friend turned rival. Recently they seemed to have mended fences, both literally and metaphorically, but Ghost didn't trust the man. He didn't know if it was his gut telling him something was off about the man, or if it was just his suspicious nature.

The back of his mind told him that if this was a club, and they were targeting the Open A Bar T because of the Souls, then that limited the prospects of who it could be. Most likely in his mind was Switchblade, the president of a club they'd been trying to take down for years, and Krissi's father. Not that she had anything to do with him. She'd been running from him when she'd ended up in Tucson and met Ruger.

He was still working through a mental list of other possibilities when his phone rang. A quick check of the screen told him it was Krissi.

"Hey," he said by way of greeting. "Thanks for getting back to me."

"No problem. I had to finish feeding Ashley, but we'll be good for a while." That's what it was. He knew there was a reason she might not be answering the phone when it rang. He'd forgotten she had the baby.

"How's the little one doing?"

"She's great, growing like a weed."

"And how's her daddy dealing with having a daughter?"

Krissi laughed. "He's getting better. He still tells her she's not allowed to date until she's thirty and no even thinking about marriage until she's at least forty-five, but he's not threatening to geld any male that even looks her way anymore."

"Give him a few years. That will probably start again when she's old enough to start flirting with boys."

"Probably," she laughed, "but baby talk isn't why you called. You're looking for information."

"I am. What do you have?"

"Not as much as I'd like, at least not yet but let me give you what I've found." She filled him in on the Kings of Destruction.

He'd made a wrong choice in dismissing the results that included Billings because it seemed this chapter was an offshoot of the one there.

Krissi gave him all the details and names she had, including someone they called Tank who was the local president. Krissi gave him more details and he wrote them down so he could use them to find out what they needed to from this Tank person. Whoever he was.

"Any more details on this Tank?" he asked once he'd taken down everything that she'd given him.

"Not a whole hell of a lot, but I do have some. I have a legal name of Bruce Walters. He has a record, not surprisingly. There are several d & d's. A couple of b & e's, one grand theft auto, one reckless endangerment, and a couple assault with a deadly weapon charges."

"Those are all charges, any convictions?"

"Just the GTA and reckless endangerment."

"What kind of time did he do?"

"Sentenced three years, released in fifteen months."

"Where?" Not that it mattered, but it might help him figure out who had sent these guys after the Souls.

"Montana State."

Ghost filed that information away and asked his next question. "How long ago?"

"A little over ten years."

"Any familiar faces serve with him?"

"I don't have that information yet. I've got a request in to find out who his cellmates were. I'm also running a search of everyone in and out the facility at the time and cross referencing it with what we know of our people of interest."

"Let me know what you find out." He didn't tell her that he suspected they'd find someone on their watch list had served time with Tank, even if they weren't cellmates. They likely knew each other and made some connection that made them reach out to him once Tuck, Ghost and some of the others came north.

He talked to her a couple minutes longer, asking about things going on in Tucson and some of his other brothers. The baby started crying in the background and Krissi had to go.

Off the phone, Ghost plugged Tank's real name into the internet to see if he could find anything more, but didn't hold his breath. It was a good thing he hadn't counted on finding more than Krissi had, because while he found a couple of newspaper articles with his name, they didn't give him any more information than he already had.

He sat at the table with his notebook and tried to figure out what he was missing, if anything. His gut said they were on the right track, the question was, did they have enough information to figure it out?

🐜

Ghost heard Malice pull into the lot and park in front of their rooms. A minute or two later the sounds of his partner letting himself into his room, vibrated through the walls. Ghost was tempted to count down and see exactly how long it took the other man to be in his room, but didn't bother. He did, however, look up from his notebook to the door joining the rooms.

Sure enough, seconds later the door was pushed open and in came Malice. He poked his head through, looking around, and grinned when he caught Ghost watching him.

The other man's grin grew as he stepped into the room and came to sit on the bed where Ghost had been earlier.

"What did you find?" Ghost asked, ignoring that Malice was waiting for him to comment on his letting himself into Ghost's room.

"The tracker is still on the truck. It's at the warehouse. There are several bikes still lined up out front under that awning, but it doesn't look like any of them have moved in days. There are also several trucks parked in the yard, a couple cars too."

"Any movement you could see?"

"There are people there. There are lights from the inside, steam coming from a couple vents. But I didn't see any movement outside. Not that I can blame anyone for staying inside when it's like this out." He gave an exaggerated shiver.

Ghost rolled his eyes and shook his head at Malice's antics.

"Did that chick call you back?"

"That chick is our treasurer's ol' lady. FYI. And I don't recommend disrespecting her in his hearing. Or hers. She'll take a layer of skin off your ears, and possibly your ass just as quick as he will."

"Good to know, but did you hear?"

"I did. Got some decent information too. Still waiting on a little more but it's a start."

He shared what he knew about Tank and his history.

"I know a couple of guys in the prison system in Montana. Let me make a couple calls and see if I can't find out a little faster."

They discussed the important information then Malice went into his room and closed the door while he reached out to his contacts. Ghost realized it was almost time for Robyn to wake up for the evening. He scheduled a few messages to be delivered a few minutes after she'd told him she got up, then made sure his volume was turned up, so he'd hear when and if she replied.

He'd moved from the table to the bed and turned on the tv when his phone chirped about half an hour later.

Robyn: I'm awake. Missed you today too, but mostly before I slept. Could have used you then. I'm going to hop in the shower, I'll be back in a bit.

Ghost stared at the message for a few seconds, wondering what she'd meant by mostly before she'd slept. Could have used him then? Did that mean what he thought it did? He remembered how badly he'd wanted to stop her from leaving. How badly he'd wanted to pull her into his lap and continue where the kiss had left off. Was that what she meant?

He could only imagine the ribbing Malice would have given him if his partner had found out about that. Ghost made a mental note not to let Malice know about Robyn if he could help it. Especially after the piece of ass comment this morning and calling Krissi a chick. He didn't know how Robyn would take such a comment, but even that one this morning had made Ghost want to rip his friend's head off.

Ghost: Sorry got distracted by the idea of what I could help you with before you went to sleep. Still half distracted. Hope you slept well.

He set the phone aside and knew he had to focus on the reason he was here in Dickenson. And it wasn't to hook up with the amazingly hot woman who worked across the street, though that was tempting.

Now that he had some information, the name of the club and who the president was, it gave him a direction. They needed to be watching this guy more closely. Another vehicle to watch from didn't hurt either.

A while later, Malice let himself back into Ghost's room and shared what he'd been able to find out. Not much new but he was able to confirm Tank's last known address was the warehouse Ghost was fairly certain was the clubhouse for these Kings of Destruction, at least from what he could tell on the online maps, it seemed to be the same building.

"We need to start watching them. Seeing what we can learn and if we can pick up any leverage on them."

"You want me to take the first shift, or you want to?"

Ghost checked the clock. If he did this right, he could cover the night shift, Malice would come relieve him, then he could go see Robyn, maybe even talk her into inviting him home with her, and Malice would be busy with the Kings and wouldn't know. That was the best way to keep from having to strangle the man for making an uncomplimentary comment.

"I'll take the first shift. I haven't been sleeping well anyway." Ghost stood and started moving around the room, gathering what he wanted to take with him for the night. "I'll take the ranch truck, since it will be dark, and it will be less likely to be recognized. You come in and find a spot with a view about 0530 in the new truck. Text me when you get in position, that way I'll know I'm in the clear to leave."

"You really think they'll be up to much at 0530?"

"We won't know unless we're watching. If I were them, and wanted to do something nefarious, I'd leave early in the morning when everyone assumed we were sleeping off the partying. Especially if my club had a reputation for partying."

Malice didn't say anything but nodded as if he hadn't considered that possibility. They'd already discussed the King's reputation for being a little wild and drinking until they started fighting or passed out.

"Are we all good?" His phone chirped and vibrated in his pocket with an incoming text, but didn't pull it out. Ghost was hoping to wait until he got into the truck to reply to Robyn.

Malice dipped his head once. "I'll let you know when I'm in place."

"If you need anything else, feel free to text. Or reach out to Lurch. He'll be able to answer as much or more than I can." Ghost grabbed the assault pack he'd shoved everything he thought he might need into, and swung it onto one shoulder. Picking up the thermos and keys, he pinned Malice with a stare.

"Make sure you lock my connecting door, so no one knows we're going back and forth, just in case housekeeping comes in, or anyone else sneaks in here while I'm out."

Malice gave him a two finger, mock salute. Ghost clenched his jaw and left. Sometimes silence was the better than picking a fight.

CHAPTER 23

Robyn got out of the shower and dressed. She found Ghost's text and replied, then took her phone with her as she went for coffee, expecting to hear from him soon, but it was a few minutes before a reply came in.

Ghost: Sorry got distracted by the idea of what I could help you with before you went to sleep. Still half distracted. Hope you slept well.

She read his message as she leaned against the counter drinking coffee and thought about what to send him next. After a moment she typed out her reply.

Robyn: Slept great. Now I'm getting ready for work. What are you plans for tonight?

Once she hit send, she set her phone down and picked up her coffee again. She spent several minutes staring out the kitchen window wondering what odd thing would pop up during tonight's shift. There was nearly always something. Her personal philosophy was that she might as well find amusement in whatever the latest drama was. It made life in general easier. And at least a little more fun. After finishing her first cup of coffee, she refilled her cup and went to finish getting ready for her shift.

She'd been working for a couple hours before she had a chance to sit down and rest for even a minute. She sat on the stool behind the counter and pulled out her phone.

Before her shift, she and Ghost had exchanged several messages and she'd heard her phone chirp a while back, but she'd been busy with a line of people coming in for gas, coffee, and other drinks as they headed into the night shift like her. There would be another almost rush, though not as big as the first people got off work and headed home, but that wouldn't be for a bit yet.

Ghost: I know you're likely busy now but let me know when you're not. I've got something going and I'll be up most of the night.

Robyn: What's going to keep you up all night?

She stared at the phone, wishing his replies would come in as quickly as you could think an answer. She could call but who knew when someone would walk in. No texting was a little slower and sometimes more irritating but better sometimes.

The door chimed, making Robyn look up. It was a single man, not quite six feet tall, but other than that and his pale skin, she couldn't tell much because of his hat and scarf.

"Good evening. Looks like it's getting colder out there," she called as she shoved her phone into her pocket.

"Evening." His voice was low and almost sullen. He turned away, toward where the coffee and soda fountains lined one wall. She kept an eye on him in case he needed anything, but didn't want him to feel watched, as if she didn't trust him or was afraid of him, so she made herself busy cleaning up the area behind the register.

"You guys carry science energy drinks?" his voice called from the rear of the room where the coolers full of sodas and energy drinks were.

"I don't think so. I've never heard of that one. Is it new?"

"X-Y-I-E-N-C-E," he spelled it. "They make several flavors and have been around for a few years. They're not as popular as Monster or have as many varieties as some of the other brands, but I like the way they taste, and they make me feel better than the others." He came her way, a couple of Rockstars in one hand. "I know you're probably not in charge of ordering, but if you drink these things, and run across them, you should try them." He set the drinks on the counter, then reached to one side and grabbed a couple of bags of candy to add to the drinks.

Robyn rang him up, bagging the items as she went. When she gave him his total, she met his gaze and found herself staring into the darkest eyes she'd ever seen. They were so dark brown they looked almost black. He'd tugged his scarf loose and she could see most of his face, with the shadow of his beard visible as if he'd shaved that morning, but that was hours ago and now you could see the stubble growth. She wondered for a moment why the man seemed so familiar, despite her being sure she'd never seen him before.

"Thanks." He took his bag and headed for the door.

"Thank you, have a good night." She waited until he was gone, and the door had completely closed behind him to pull her phone back out. She couldn't remember if it had chirped an incoming message or not.

Ghost: Watching the guys who have been harassing us at the ranch. Unless there's some reason not to, I'll probably be here all night.

Robyn frowned at her phone as she typed her reply.

Robyn: Why at night? Aren't they home for the night?

She assumed that since they'd spent several weeks in Wyoming causing trouble for Ghost and his friends, that they didn't have jobs, or at least not jobs that kept them busy this time of year.

Ghost: They're hanging around a warehouse I assume is the clubhouse. I need to watch in case they go home or to figure out who the leader is.

Ghost: I meant to ask you. Ever heard of anyone called Tank?

Robyn: Good luck. I hear the temperature is dropping fast out there. You may be in for a cold night.

She sent that message first and tried to remember if she'd ever heard of anyone going by Tank, or if she'd met him, but she didn't think so.

Robyn: Tank doesn't sound familiar, but I'll keep thinking about it.

The name bounced around in her head for a while, but didn't bring anything to mind. Then it dawned on her. If anyone would know about Tank, it would be Dad. He hadn't been with the Stark County Sheriff's Office for a few years, but he still had friends on the force, and he might have heard at least rumors.

A glance at the clock told her might be up still, but she didn't want to call, in case he's already gone to bed. She sent a text instead.

Robyn: Hey, you know anything about a guy around here called Tank?

She didn't have to wait long, because his response came in less than five minutes later.

Dad: I've heard of him. How did you encounter him?

Robyn: I haven't. A friend asked if I'd ever heard of him.

Dad: You know I don't like to tell you what to do, but someone looking for him would be a good person to stay away from.

Robyn: Even if they're not looking to get involved with him but to find out why his men are following his friends around?

Dad: I'd need to know more to be sure, but Tank and his men are bad news. As in people disappear around them bad news.

Robyn's heart thundered in her chest knowing that this Tank was that kind of bad news and that his group was already causing problems for Ghost and his friends. She thought about it for a few minutes. Should she pass what Dad said on to Ghost? She'd asked so she could tell him, but what would he make of the information? What would he think of her asking Dad?

Robyn shook her head and typed up the message. She had asked Dad so Ghost could know. It would defeat the purpose if she didn't pass on the information. And now Dad would worry about her even more. She hated that part, but she'd find a way to set his mind at ease.

Robyn: Asked my dad, he's former SCSO. Says Tank is bad news. Ugly bad news.

She hit send. Again, she wished messages came back and forth as quickly as you could think them. She wanted to know what Ghost was thinking, that he would be careful when dealing with this Tank person. She wanted him to say it wasn't worth it and leave but she knew he couldn't; not if this guy was as bad as Dad said, which Robyn didn't doubt, or that he was doing what Ghost had told her and harassing the women around the ranch.

Her hands shook as she thought about what these men could have done to them in place of just following them around and scaring them. Was that all they had done?

Robyn's phone rang, startling her. The screen said it was Ghost.

"Hello?" She fought to keep what she was feeling from her voice.

"Hey, you okay to talk for a few minutes?"

"I'm good for a while, unless someone comes in."

"Good. Let me know if you need to go."

"Alright." Hearing how steady his voice was made her stomach settle and her heart began to slow.

"I need to ask you a few questions and this was faster."

"Okay." She frowned, wondering what kind of questions he had.

"You said SCSO, I assume that's the sheriff's office, right?"

"Yeah, Stark County."

"Is that the county we're in now?"

"Yeah." It hadn't occurred to her he wouldn't already know that.

"Did your dad say if he'd ever encountered Tank himself?"

Robyn shook her head then realized he couldn't see her. "No, but he said he'd heard of him."

"Good to know. How long ago did your dad leave the sheriff's office?"

She wrinkled up her nose, trying to remember when exactly he'd left. "Four, maybe five years."

"Good to know. Thanks for asking for me. It helps to know the local law enforcement doesn't think much of him." Ghost was quiet for a moment. "Hang on a second. I've got some movement here."

She heard movement on the other end of the line, but she couldn't tell what it was. The longer the quiet stretched, the more her stomach churned. Hoping nothing would go wrong. Hoping he hadn't been spotted. Hoping Ghost wouldn't end up hurt.

It seemed like an eon had passed but the clock on the wall told her it had been less than two minutes.

"Sorry that took so long. I'm back."

The sound of Ghost's voice coming across the phone line made Robyn glad she was sitting down. Her shoulders slumped and her whole body felt weak. She was sure if she'd been standing her knees would have given out with relief.

"Is everything okay?" She struggled to keep the fear she'd been feeling from making her voice shake, but wasn't entirely sure she'd managed.

"Everything is fine. One of the men came outside and took a piss outside the building." His disgust was clear in his voice.

Robyn couldn't help but crinkle her nose. How would the place smell if they did that regularly?

"Are you going to be warm enough sitting there all night? I hope you're at least in the cab of your truck."

"I am in the truck, and I'll be fine. I've got good insulation, some heat packs for my clothes and a thermos of coffee."

"Oh." She forgot to try to hide the disappointment in her voice. Until he mentioned it, she hadn't even thought about him coming into get his usual thermos of coffee.

"I would have come and gotten my coffee from you, but I was already here when you started your shift. You did start at the same time as last night, right?"

"I did."

"I thought so, that means you'll get off about the same time in the morning too, right?"

"It does." She was starting to see where he was going with this. Did he want breakfast again?

"Good. Malice will have relieved me by then. I was hoping maybe I could cook you breakfast."

Heat fluttered through her. She liked the idea of him cooking for her, but where? "In your motel room? I didn't know those have kitchens."

His low chuckle seemed to vibrate across the phone, making the flutters turn liquid and pool low in her belly.

"They don't. I was hoping maybe I could talk you into letting me cook at your place."

A slow smile crept across her face as she imagined Ghost in her kitchen. The chime of the door alarm drew her attention. "I've got to go. I'll get back to you."

CHAPTER 24

Ghost couldn't resist checking his phone every few seconds for a new message from Robyn. As if it wouldn't alert him. He knew better but he was eager to hear back from her. His offer to cook for her at her place. Would she take it the way he'd meant it? Or would she assume he was just trying to get her into bed?

Finally, after what seemed like an eternity, his phone buzzed in his hand.

Robyn: Breakfast sounds great. And my place would work.

He was trying to decide how best to reply when another message popped up on the screen.

Robyn: And it will make it convenient for what I'd like to do afterward.

Robyn: Get to know you better.

Ghost stared at the phone for several seconds trying to decide what to say next. After a moment he glanced up at the warehouse he was 99% certain housed the Kings of Destruction clubhouse, just to make sure nothing had changed then looked back to his phone.

Ghost: I want to get to know you better too.

He didn't put that he wanted to get to know her better not just personally but physically too. From the way she'd kissed him that morning, he could only hope she meant the same. But he was not going to ask, not over text.

Hell, he wasn't crass enough to say it even in person. At least not to her. He could be crass and rude, when he wanted to, but never with someone who's good side he was trying to get onto.

The phone buzzed in his hand again, pulling his thoughts away from where they'd begun to wander.

Robyn: Do you want to meet me at my place? Are you going to need to stop by your room first?

He thought about it a second. Meeting her there only made sense. She wouldn't want to leave her car at work all day, and what could he need from his room? He glanced down at himself in the dark. Maybe a quick shower after sitting in this truck all night. And a quick stop at a grocery wouldn't be a bad idea, to make sure he had the stuff he wanted to cook for her.

Ghost: Meeting you would be great. And yeah, I'd like to stop by my room. Any food allergies I need to be aware of?

He forced himself not to watch the screen while he waited for her reply, instead he kept his eyes on the warehouse. Criminy, this was the most boring job he'd had in a long time. Even worse than watching the men sit beside the road every day back in Wyoming. At least then he didn't have to worry about noise. He could turn the radio on and sing along when he needed help staying awake. Now, he could text but reading the news or something else would keep him from being able to watch the warehouse.

He made a mental note to pick up some kind of headphones in the morning. He hadn't thought to get some before now and wanted to smack himself for the oversight.

His phone buzzed again, and he could help the grin that spread across his face as he wondered what Robyn had to say now.

When he popped up his messages, he found this one wasn't from Robyn, as he'd assumed. It was from Krissi.

Krissi: Found more details for you. Check your email.

She wouldn't have sent anything to his general email, so Ghost went through the extra security and steps to pull up his secure email. There he found a message from the club treasurer's wife. In it was a list of facts and details about Tank and some of the other members of the Kings here in North Dakota. There were bios, including pictures of several members, though she'd cautioned him that it wasn't an exhaustive list. He could have already told her that from the faces he'd seen moving in and out of the clubhouse before it got dark and since. He scanned through the message, looking for anything that might help him tonight, while continuing to glance up and make sure there was nothing new happening across the street.

He scanned all the way through the message and closed it, planning to go through it better, absorbing what he could and asking for more information here and there, tomorrow when he had more time. Now, in the dark, wasn't the best time to review all the details that had been included. He looked back to the warehouse, considering some of the details of the information Krissi had sent him, the bits that had stuck in his mind.

His phone chirped again. A glance told him it was Robyn. He couldn't help smiling as he opened the message.

Robyn: No allergies, here's my address.

The next message held her address and a couple smiley faces. They texted back and forth most of the night, but Ghost's mind kept going back to Krissi's email and what it might mean.

She hadn't yet found a link from Tank to anyone they knew had a beef against the Souls. That didn't mean it wasn't there, only that it wasn't obvious, and they hadn't found it yet. He would give her a few days and see if she turned up anything more. Then he would confront the man and see what he could learn.

CHAPTER 25

Robyn spent the rest of her shift exchanging fun texts with Ghost in between customers. She looked forward to each message and it made her shift go faster than even reading did. Though she wasn't sure if that was because she was enjoying the texting or because she was looking forward to having him come cook for her once she got off.

And what she hoped to do after breakfast. She had some ideas, but she wasn't ready to ask him what his intentions were. She didn't want to scare him off if all he was after was a fling while he was in Dickenson. Though, after his asking what it would take to get her to leave here, maybe that wasn't what he was after.

Once she got off work, she swung by the grocery store where she'd encountered the guy who had been so sure Robyn knew where 'she' was. She hoped this visit wasn't so exciting, but she had a few things she wanted to pick up.

Ten minutes later, she dumped a dozen or so items on the belt, so far un-accosted, and glanced up to find Bobby as her cashier.

"Hey, morning girl call in sick again?" she asked as the items on the belt moved closer to him and she moved around to the small shelf that held the card machine so she could put in her phone number for the discounts.

"No call, no show." He started ringing up her items. "How was your day?"

"Quiet, which is good. No drunks insisting I sell to them even though we don't carry alcohol, or demanding to know where it's hidden. No one trying to sneak shit out as if they didn't just walk right past me with it. I'll take a quiet night over either of those any day."

"Glad you had a quiet shift."

"Are you going to be stuck on the register all day?" Robyn asked after he gave her the total. She paid while he started bagging her purchase.

"No, I've got another coming in in twenty minutes, then a couple more right behind her. I'm only stuck here for a little bit." He finished bagging her items and set the bags up on the end of the counter so she could pick them up.

"Glad to hear you'll have help soon. Have a good day, Bobby." She took her bags and headed for the door.

"You too, sleep well," he called after her.

She nodded then went out to the car. Her mind already back at her place, hoping she hadn't spent too much time in the store and would still make it before Ghost got there.

✤

She breathed a sigh of relief when she got to the house and Ghost's pickup wasn't parked out front. She parked, hurried inside, and wondered if she should push her luck and try for a shower.

After a moment's thought she decided not to try it, instead she hurried through the house scrambling to pick up anything left out of place so Ghost wouldn't think she was a total slob. Not that she thought he would judge her housekeeping, but who knew what anyone would do when they came into a new place.

First, she put away her purchases, mostly in the kitchen but there were a couple she tucked into the nightstand drawer, then she tackled the living room. When she was finished with the main room, she moved on to the bedroom and then on to the kitchen. It had the least needing to be done as she routinely loaded her breakfast dishes before leaving for work.

She was wiping all the counters off to be sure they were all clean and ready for him when the doorbell rang. She hurried to drape the cloth over the edge of the sink then went to answer the door.

Ghost stood on the doorstep, scowling down at her.

"Did you just open the door without checking to be sure who it was?"

Robyn rolled her eyes, took his hand, and tugged him inside. Once she wouldn't hit him with the door, she closed it, leaving the cold wind outside and enveloping them in the comfortable warmth of the house.

"How was your night?" She ignored his question and started with one of her own.

His eyes narrowed but his scowl eased. "Fine."

"Learn anything helpful?"

101

"Not really."

He seemed to be letting it go. Good. She'd learned that tactic when dealing with Dad and his overprotective tendencies.

"Sorry to hear that." She stretched up and kissed his cheek, hoping he might take the invitation and kiss her back, but no luck. Instead, she sank back to the pads of her feet and smiled up at him. "Come on into the kitchen." She led him into the kitchen, not looking to see if he followed. "Coffee?" she asked as she turned to find him several steps behind her. He'd stopped to kick off his boots before following her.

"Sure." He glanced around the room, his gaze settling on her again. "But don't make a pot just for me. I can drink water."

"I have some other things, too." She went to the fridge and opened the door. "I have coke, tea and milk too."

He chuckled. "Is the tea sweet?"

"No, but we can add sugar if you want."

Ghost gave his head a single shake. "Unsweetened is fine."

Robyn fixed him a glass and handed it to him.

"Thank you," he said. He took a sip then set it on the counter beside him. "I've been thinking about doing this all night." He hooked one arm around her waist and tugged her close.

Robyn stared up at him, her breath seemed to hang in her throat and her heart thundered in her ears as she watched his mouth move closer.

Ghost's mouth covered hers in a brief, searing kiss. She couldn't help the way her hands came up to cup his arms. Her fingers curled, gripping his triceps, and tugging him closer. She wanted to feel him against her, his skin brushing against hers. A groan escaped from her throat as he pulled away and broke the kiss. She wanted to pull him back to kiss him longer, to feel the slid of his tongue over hers. But she didn't. Instead, she backed away, waiting to see what he would do.

"Worth the wait." His soft words made her glance up to find his eyes as hot as her body felt. "And it will be worth waiting more. Let's see about food first. What do you want to eat?" He'd been so eager to see her again he'd forgotten to stop by the store. He was mentally kicking himself for that now.

"What can you cook?" She couldn't help the low chuckle that escaped as she stepped back.

"I can manage a few things, assuming you've got the ingredients. Mind if I look?" He motioned toward the fridge.

"Help yourself. Do you want me as an audience, or can I go take a shower?"

"I don't need an audience, but tell me where a few things are first." He asked about cooking utensils and pans.

She gave him instructions on where to find them, and to where her spice cabinet was. "If you need anything else, feel free to look. I'll hurry so it doesn't get cold." She couldn't resist stopping beside him and stretching up to steal another steaming kiss, though she wished it had lasted longer, then went for the shower.

CHAPTER 26

Ghost fought to keep the grin off his face as Robyn sauntered out of the kitchen. He didn't bother to try to resist watching the way her ass swung from side to side with each step.

Damn that woman did things to him. He shifted himself in his jeans and couldn't help but think of some of the things he'd like her to do to him. Later, he reminded himself, as she disappeared around a corner. He turned back to what he was supposed to be doing, fixing breakfast for them both.

Trying to focus on his task instead of imagining her naked and wet in the shower, he opened the fridge to find that not only did she have bacon, she also had sausage. He grabbed the tube of sausage, the eggs, bell peppers, an onion and a stick of butter then turned back to the counter. Since he was going to cook, he might as well do it right.

Twenty minutes later, as he was getting ready to pour the eggs into the skillet and start the omelets, Robyn came back into the room. The soft scent of lavender and lilacs wafted by as she stepped past him.

"Find everything all right?" She went to the refrigerator, pulled out the milk jug and turned to face him. "Wow did you. You've been busy."

Ghost glanced up to watch her eyes go wide as she took in what he'd been doing while she was gone. He looked down at the counter and stove then back up at her.

"Too much?"

"Not at all. I was expecting eggs, maybe bacon, not all this." She waved a hand over the counter.

Ghost looked back down. That was what he'd done, well not bacon but sausage. He'd sliced half of it and cooked it in patty's then browned the rest in case she wanted it in her omelet, then diced the peppers and onion, and shredded some of the cheddar he'd found in a drawer in the fridge. It was all ready for him to make her eggs however she liked them. He might have chopped more than they needed but it would all keep and could be used in a lot of things.

"I got caught up in what I was doing. Do you prefer scrambled or omelets? And what do you want in them?"

She gave a long blink and a slow shake of her head. "Omelet with cheese and peppers, sausage patty on the side."

"Two or three eggs?"

"Three, please." She tugged a stool from the end of the counter where he'd seen it sitting earlier, sat and watched him. "You look at home in the kitchen. You cook a lot?"

"Not anymore, but I used to cook a lot of what I ate."

"Why not anymore?"

"Meals are included at the ranch. Between London and Kerry, they make sure we have three meals a day, and there's plenty of other things around in case we get hungry."

"You cooked for yourself before that?"

Ghost glanced up. "I did. It's difficult to eat out every meal and still stay in shape, especially if you don't want to spend every spare hour working out." He lifted one shoulder in dismissal. "I had things I wanted to do more than spend my life in a gym." He didn't say that a chunk of that was chasing women. She didn't need to hear that. Nor did she need to know how much time he spent at the range. He glanced back up at her in time to see her skim her eyes down his body and back up again.

"I can see why that might be an issue. I must say, you've done a great job of staying in shape."

A coy smile curved her full lip, making Ghost want to leave the food where it was and kiss her. From there he wanted it to progress to more, a lot more.

But he fought to keep his desire from his eyes. He shifted on his feet, so his growing erection was a touch less painful and less obvious. It wasn't that he didn't want Robyn to know how much he wanted her, but timing was a thing. He'd learned that the hard way over the years.

"Thanks. I like the way you look too." He shot her a wink and a grin as he finished her omelet, slid it on to a plate and set it on the counter in front of her before adding his own eggs to the skillet. While he waited for them to start setting so he could add his filling, he set the plate with sausage next to hers so she could help herself. "Dig in."

Robyn shook her head. "I'll wait for you. We can eat together."

"They'll get cold." He shot her a scowl.

"Not that cold." She waved her fingers toward the stove, as if telling him to mind his own eggs, not hers.

He shook his head and turned back to the skillet, where it was time to add his onions, peppers, sausage, and cheese. After adding his fillings, he flipped the edges and waited a few more seconds before turning the entire thing. When it was done, he slid it onto a plate, made sure the burner was off and turned back to Robyn. "Where do you want to eat?"

"In here." She led him to a small, four-seater table in a dining room hadn't noticed.

"This is a nice little room. I didn't even notice it here."

"I love the light it gets in the morning," she motioned to the window along the east wall, "but I don't come in here as often as I should. Especially not this time of year. Between few hours of daylight and working nights, I haven't had the time to do it justice." She turned her attention to her food. They both ate and for a few minutes the only sounds were the soft clink of flatware against their dishes.

After she'd cleaned her plate, Robyn sat back in her chair and a smiled at him. He couldn't help but notice how relaxed she seemed.

"That was really good. Thank you for cooking for me."

"Not a problem, I enjoyed a chance to get in the kitchen again. It's been several months since I had the chance."

"Oh? You haven't been working for the ranch very long?"

"My buddy inherited it a few months ago. Some friends and I came up to help him out, get settled in and stuff. I decided I liked it up here and wanted to stay a little longer. Then these guys started harassing our women and wouldn't stop when we warned them off."

"Have you figured out what's going on yet?" The frown marring her forehead made him want to smooth it away and change the subject, so she didn't have anything to worry about, but he knew that was foolish.

"Not yet, but we're getting closer. The information you were able to share about Tank helped." Not a whole lot, but some and that was what he wanted to share with her now.

"I'm glad." She stood and picked up her plate. "You done?"

Ghost nodded, she picked up his plate and carried it into the kitchen. He stayed where he was for a brief moment then got up and followed. He would let her put away the leftover food, but he was going to help her clean up his mess. He'd learned a long time ago, one of the easiest ways to seduce a woman was to let her see him clean up after himself.

After the breakfast mess had been cleaned up, Robyn invited him into the living room to relax a bit.

"We can find something to watch if you want. There's not much but news and talk shows this time of day, but I've got a couple streaming services. I'm sure we can find something." She seemed nervous as she sat next to him on the sofa. As if not sure what to say or do next.

Ghost didn't have any such doubts.

"I'm good. I like just talking to you. But there's something I want to do even more."

"What?" She looked up, eyes wide.

He didn't think it was innocence in her look, maybe surprise?

"Lean over here."

She did as he asked, he lifted her chin with the tip of one finger and lowered his head slowly, giving her a chance to move away or tell him no.

Robyn didn't move away. He covered her mouth with his, starting out soft, then coaxing her lips apart with his tongue.

Her groan tore at his control. He fought to keep things slow to keep from scaring her. When she lifted his hand and placed it on her breast, he struggled to keep from becoming too aggressive. Instead, he cupped the mound, glad to find the only restriction was the sweatshirt she'd pulled on after her shower. No bra to keep him from being able to tease the tip or enjoy the roundness filling his palm.

Her hand slid along his waist, finding its way under his shirt, and setting his skin on fire. He groaned as her hand skimmed up his belly to tease his nipple. Ghost couldn't help pouring more of his desire, his need, into the kiss. She shifted, moving closer. His hand on her tit seemed to bounce and wobble for a moment. She broke the kiss.

Ghost watched as she moved onto her hands and knees then crawled toward him, stopping only when she was almost sitting in his lap.

"That's better." Robyn wedged her hands under his shirt again and slid them along his skin, shoving his shirt up as they went. He reached behind his head and tugged the shirt off in one swift motion.

Her heavy-lidded eyes watched as he tossed the bundle of cloth aside then turned back to him. He hesitated to touch more than what he could see. He didn't want her to think he was trying to take more than she was offering, even if she didn't seem to hesitate to ask for what she wanted. He liked that she'd become aggressive in seeking what she wanted.

Especially when what she wanted was exactly what he wanted too. He let his hands drift to her tits, playing and kneading them over the sweatshirt she was wearing. He let his fingers flick back and forth over her taut nipples. Robyn arched into his touch, a low growl crawling from her throat.

"Come on. Let's go somewhere a little more comfortable."

She stood, took his hand, and tugged him off the couch. He let her pull him to her feet, then followed as she led him down a short hall and through a doorway into what was obviously her bedroom.

"Looks like you're way ahead of me."

She tugged the hem of her shirt up and over her head revealing he'd been right. All she had on beneath the sweatshirt was the knit pajama pants covering her legs. And if she wasn't wearing a bra, what were the odds of her not wearing any panties either?

He let his gaze play down her body and a smile curve his lips as he thanked the heaven he'd thought ahead enough to leave his pistol in the truck.

CHAPTER 27

Now that she'd gotten him into her bedroom, Robyn was thrilled. Things were going just as she'd hoped and judging from the look on Ghost's face after she'd peeled her shirt off, he was on board and planning to take this exactly where she wanted it to go.

"Come on. I want to get to know you better." She grabbed his belt and tugged him closer as she stretched up to kiss him again.

Ghost caught one hand and pulled it away from his belt, she let it slide along his middle as she lost herself in the heat of his kiss. His hands played across her skin. A trail of fire lit the path of his fingertips until his palms cupped her breasts and squeezed. She let her eyes drift closed and a whimper escape her throat.

"Too rough? Did I hurt you?"

"Not at all. It feels amazing. The contrast of gentle and rough is just right."

"I'm glad." He smoothed his thumb along the side of one breast as he slid his hand around the curve of her waist to her back and tugged her against him. She trailed the tip of her tongue along his collar bone, then dipped to tease his nipple with her tongue and teeth. His fingers curled into her waist, tugging her close and letting her know he enjoyed her ministrations.

It didn't take long for her to get lost in his touch. Their clothing seemed to melt away and Robyn didn't know if he knew the right places to touch her and how, but it seemed that way.

In no time he'd laid her back on the bed and kissed his way down her torso. As he looked up at her from between her thighs, she fought the urge to bury her fingers in that lush red hair and show him just where she needed his mouth. Instead, she bit her lip and curled her fists into the sheets.

Ghost paused what he was doing, making her want to scream not to stop.

"None of that, sunshine. No hurting yourself. I want to hear every whimper and cry that escapes that pretty mouth of yours."

"What you're going to hear is a scream of frustration if you stop now."

"Oh, I'm not stopping." He did something with his fingers that made her breath catch. "But I don't want you biting your lip. I want to hear you call out. I want you to tell me what you need."

"Yes, sir."

"We can play that way if you like."

She wanted to ask what he meant but he lowered his head back between her thighs and all thoughts of play and meanings flew from her head.

"There, right there. Harder. Yes. Oh yes. That's it..." her directions trailed off into a wordless scream as sensation overwhelmed her and pleasure flooded her every sense. Her entire body seemed to seize. Every muscle tensed and the only thought running through her mind was *DAMN*.

When Robyn had come back to her senses enough to realize she was the only one who'd gotten off, she also realized Ghost was laying beside her, his head propped up on one hand as he watched her, grinning.

"I bet that wasn't what you were hoping for," she said as she rolled to face him.

"Not exactly, but I'm not complaining. You look amazing when you come, sunshine. That glow around you gets brighter. Bright enough to make even the sun dim in comparison."

Robyn didn't know what to say, so she didn't. She let her hands talk for her. She smoothed one hand along his chest. Tracing the outline of one of the tattoos. A pair of stylized Ss that looked almost like twin lightning bolts on the right size of his chest. She'd have to ask about them later. Now, she had other things in mind.

She let her hand trail down his body until her fingers dipped below the waist of his boxers and found what she was after. The hard length of him.

Wrapping her hand around his cock, she lowered her lips to his chest and began tracing it along the same path her fingers had taken. She wanted to return the favor, though she wasn't about to let things end there. She wanted to feel the thick rod her fingers were currently wrapped around, buried deep inside her.

"You don't have to." His voice was deeper and rougher than normal as his hand wrapped around her arm to stop her downward momentum.

"Do you not want me to?"

"Fuck yes, I want it. But I don't want you to feel like you have to."

"I know I don't have to. I want to. But I want more too." She let a teasing smile curve her lips as she continued down the path she'd started along. Licking and nipping her way down his stomach, then pushing the waistband of his boxers down to reveal her goal. The long, thick length of him with more than a couple of inches protruding above the top of her fist.

She couldn't resist the temptation of watching him through her lashes as she swirled her tongue around the tip, just teasing him to start. The way his breath caught encouraged her. She couldn't help watching his face as she engulfed his cock all the way down to the top of her fist in her mouth.

Ghost's eyes seemed to roll back in his head.

"Fuck, sunshine. That feels so fucking good." He slid his hand up and down her back, encouraging her. She thought he might want to bury his hand in her hair and guide her to do what he wanted but he didn't. She liked that he didn't. She teased him for a few minutes then backed off, releasing his cock from both her mouth and her hand. Then moved up to kiss him.

She loved tasting herself on his lips and tongue and lost herself in the kiss, in his hands on her body, for a moment, then remembered what she was doing. Breaking free, Robyn reached for the nightstand where she'd put the condoms earlier when she'd gotten home, and took a string from the box. She could only be thankful she'd had the forethought to open it as she'd put it in the drawer as she didn't have the patience to fight with it now.

She fumbled with the packet, trying to tear it open but failing. Frustration had her nearly putting the thing between her teeth, despite knowing it was a big no-no, when Ghost plucked the small foil packet from her fingers.

"Let me." He gave her a lopsided grin as he easily tore the packet open. "You want to do the honors, or you want me to?"

Robyn plucked the thing from his fingers and ran the tip of her tongue along her lips, just to tease him. Then she straddled his thighs, and sitting on her heels, focused on unrolling the protection down his length. Making a point to bite her lip as if it took more concentration that it should, glancing up at Ghost through her lashes to see if he was noticing or if she was being silly simply for her own amusement.

"You got it," his voice rumbled through her, "now come up here and let me bite that lip instead of you. I'm sure it's more fun when I'm doing it."

Well, he had a point there. She leaned forward, sliding her hands up his body as she went, bracing herself on his chest as she leaned in and stretched up for a kiss. Why did his kisses cloud her mind and make her want more? She didn't know the whys, only that it they did. When she couldn't wait any longer, she broke the kiss and lifted herself onto her knees. She lined her opening up with his cock and lowered herself down over him.

Robyn used her weight to drive her down onto him. Unable to resist, she let her head fall back and a groan of happiness escape her throat as his thick cock filled her. It only took a few seconds until her hips met his. She wanted to stay like this, but she needed more, and she knew he did too. Unable to resist the temptation, she started rocking her hips while she slid her hands up her own torso, pausing a moment to cup her breasts and tease her nipples before moving up her neck then running her fingers through her hair. Once finished, she picked up his hands where they lay on the bed to either side of them and set them on her hips before moving her own hands to tease his nipple and caress across his chest.

As she leaned forward to tease him, she let her legs do more of the work, rocking her back and forth, driving him in and out of her. Ghost's hands began to roam.

"Oh, yeah. Like that," she said when his hands reached her breasts. "Squeeze them harder." Her breath came in rougher pants. She lost track of time, the world narrowing to the two of them and the sensations of their bodies coming together. Her muscles clenched.

"You're so sweet." Ghost leaned up to tease one nipple with his lips and tongue, his teeth scraped the tip.

Robyn gasped. "Bite it."

"You sure?"

"Bite it, please." Her words were little more than air, but she needed it. So bad.

She felt the edge of his teeth as he set them in the sensitive skin of her areola and bit down, gently at first then with growing pressure.

The pleasure hit her all at once. She didn't stop moving but her head fell back, a scream ripped itself from her as nearly every muscle in her body clenched. But he wasn't coming yet, she couldn't stop.

Before she knew what was happening, his teeth loosened on her breast an arm wrapped around her waist and the world was moving.

It seemed to only take the blink of an eye, but Robyn knew it had to have been longer. She blinked up at Ghost, now above her, moving inside her. This wasn't what she'd had in mind, but she had no complaints. Instead, she slid her hands along his chest then wrapped her fingers around his biceps.

Ghost drove into her with a single-minded intensity that had pleasure washing through her in no time. Without thinking about it, her legs wrapped around his hips. She found herself shaking and begging for more.

She lost count of the number of times sensation and need overwhelmed her every sense. Only that by the time they both collapsed, limp and sated, she could barely speak for gasping for air.

It took several minutes before either of them were able to stir, but they cleaned up and climbed back into bed. Ghost lay on his back and Robyn curled into his side, her head resting on his shoulder as if they'd been sleeping this way for years.

Her last thought as she drifted off to sleep was to wonder if he'd still be there when she woke.

CHAPTER 28

Achirp from his phone woke Ghost. He was instantly awake and aware of where he was, and couldn't help but smile at the way Robyn curled up against him. But he didn't want the phone to chirp again and wake her, so he carefully disentangled himself and slid from the bed, murmuring softly that he would be right back when she gave a sleepy protest.

He tugged on his jeans, slipped from the room, and pulled his phone from the pocket. Checking his alerts, he found a message from Malice.

Malice: I've got movement. Who do you want me to tail? The ones we followed up here or this Tank?

Ghost didn't even have to think about that, and realized he should have told Malice before he'd left him alone this morning.

Ghost: Tank. We need to figure out where we can get him alone to ask him a few questions.

Malice didn't need to know until it happened that they might have to resort to creative questioning techniques. It wasn't that he thought Malice would object to them. He knew from experience Malice could handle whatever they needed to do. Ghost didn't want to draw him that deep into the workings of the Souls unless he had to. Not until more of his brothers had met him, and Malice had a better idea of if he wanted to become a Soul or if he wanted to just be a ranch hand.

Malice: Will do. When you relieving me?

Ghost checked the clock. It was barely one. He'd only had a few hours sleep.

Ghost: Around 1800. I'll be in touch to find out where you are.

He set an alarm so he'd get up in time, then went back to join Robyn in bed. He shed his jeans and slid into bed beside her, shaking his head at how she'd curled into tiny ball, as if trying to stay warm with him gone. How did she sleep when she was alone? Ghost curled around her, tugging her into his arms. She snuggled into him and let out a contented sigh. An odd sense of rightness washed through Ghost as he drifted off to sleep.

When his phone alarm went off, Ghost shut it off as quickly as he could, hoping not to disturb Robyn and let her get at least a little more sleep. He slipped out of bed and grabbed his clothes, searching for his shirt for a moment before remembering he'd taken it off in the living room the night before.

He took his clothes out into the living room and dressed quickly, wishing he could wake her up with food and coffee, but he had to get moving or Malice would get suspicious. The last thing he wanted was Malice to start his picking and teasing of Robyn instead of just him. Just the idea of his friend harassing her made him see red. He hadn't liked when these Kings assholes were harassing the women around the ranch, and if the idea of his friend doing it to Robyn made him this irrationally angry, how would he feel if it was the Kings harassing Robyn?

It was a good thing they hadn't so far, because they might not survive such a mistake. He slipped out of Robyn's house and to the truck, making sure to lock her door as he left. In the truck he texted Malice to find out where he was, then while he waited, sent Robyn a text.

Ghost: Sorry I had to leave. I had to relieve my buddy on watch duty. Wish I could have been there to kiss you awake.

He hit send and started the truck so it would start warming up, and a message came in from Malice with an address Ghost didn't recognize. Thank God for phones with GPS and navigation.

Thirty minutes after he left Robyn's place, Ghost pulled into an empty space in front of a home two doors down from the address Malice had given him as where Tank had been for the last several hours. He killed the engine, shifted in his seat so he could see the house in question, then turned his screen brightness all the way down so the glow from his screen wouldn't give away that he was sitting there and texted Malice that he was in place.

Malice: Good. I'm going to get out of here, but once I'm back to the motel I'll call so I can update you.

Ghost: 10-4

He was still waiting for Malice to call or someone to move at Tank's place when his phone chirped with the tone that he'd set for Robyn, so he'd know when it was her.

Robyn: Missed you when I woke up. Knew it wasn't likely, but I wish you'd been there.

Ghost remembered the warmth of her in his arms all day, then took a deep breath, remembering the way she'd smelled. His cock stirred at the memory of her touch, not to mention the way she tasted.

Ghost: I wanted to be there. Wanted to wake you with a kiss, maybe more.

Ghost: You looked so sweet, I hated to disturb you.

Ghost: But I'd already stolen enough of your sleep, so I let you sleep while I went to work. Have a good night at work.

He finished typing his last message, hit send and turned his attention back to Tank's house. Still no movement. He wasn't looking forward to another night in the cold, but taking the night shift was worth it if he got to spend his days with Robyn.

CHAPTER 29

Robyn couldn't help the pang of disappointment that washed through her when she woke alone, though she hadn't expected him to still be there, she'd hoped. After getting up and going through her morning routine, she made her way into the kitchen and started coffee, then picked up her phone to see if anyone had called while she slept.

That's when she found the text Ghost had sent when he left. Warmth spread through her chest as she read it, noting that he'd sent it less than an hour before her alarm had gone off. She sent him a message back then went to finish getting dressed.

By the time she was ready for more food, there were several messages waiting from Ghost. She couldn't stop the odd flutter in her stomach that seeing that he'd responded, not once but several times gave her. It made her feel like he cared. Did he love her? Obviously not, it was way too soon for that. She couldn't even say what exactly she felt for him, other than want, but she knew something was growing.

Robyn checked her phone again before leaving for work and found she'd somehow missed an incoming message.

Ghost: Yes, I'll up all night again. I'd be happy to chat when you have time.

Ghost: Maybe see you again once we're both through with work. If you're up for that.

Robyn: I'd love to see you after work in the morning. I'm headed in to work now, it will be a bit, but I'll text when I have a few minutes. Stay safe.

She stared at the screen for several seconds after hitting send, wondering if it was too much. After a moment she shrugged and shoved her phone into her pocket. The message was gone, it was too late to pull it back or change it so why worry about it now? She gathered the last of her things and made her way out to her car. It was time to get to work.

Robyn had been at work for a couple hours before things slowed down enough for her to sit down a second and check her messages. Sure enough, as she'd expected there were a couple from Ghost.

Ghost: Thinking about you.

Ghost: Remembering from this morning is making it hard to sit and do my job.

Ghost: I'm having a hard time focusing on what I'm supposed to be doing. My mind keeps wandering to what you looked like this morning. Stretched out on the bed. Wrapped around my cock. Coming around my cock.

Her face heated and she quickly looked around to make sure no one had come in and could see her. Relieved she was alone, she let her phone rest on her lap for a moment or two while she thought about what to say.

Robyn: I had fun last night too. Would love to repeat it. You going to be busy when I get off work?

She hit send and stared at the screen for several seconds before shaking her head and shoving it in her pocket. She needed to keep busy or waiting to hear from him was going to drive her crazy.

The chimes above the door rang, drawing her attention. She went back to work, forgetting to fret about Ghost and what he might say next.

By the time her shift ended, Robyn was dead on her feet. There had been one customer after another nearly all night long. She'd only had a few chances to sit down and rest, much less think about anything but work all night long. As she made her way out to her car, she remembered she'd never gotten back to Ghost. When she reached the car, she started the engine and heater then pulled out her phone.

There was no new message from him. The message she'd sent the night before hadn't even been read.

That was odd. He usually read her messages right away. Was he not as eager to see her again as he'd seemed? Had something happened to keep him from getting back to her?

She looked across the street at the motel where he was staying, but didn't see his truck parked anywhere. She had no clue what room he was in or where his friend, Malice, was. If Ghost was supposed to be off when she got off, wouldn't Malice already be there to relieve him? Was there anything she could do?

She didn't see anything. She didn't know enough about him or who he worked for. With one more scan of the parking lot across the street, she put her car in gear and headed home.

CHAPTER 30

Ghost kept his eyes on Tank's place but listened for the alert on his phone. He didn't know how long he'd been watching, waiting for something to happen, only that it had been a while. But Robyn was usually busy for the beginning of her shift. It took longer for her to respond early in the evening rather than in the wee hours of then night.

Between being lost in his thoughts and watching Tank's house he was startled when someone stepped up beside the driver's window where he sat and knocked on the glass.

Ghost's heart thundered in his chest as he turned to find one of the men that he'd seen at the clubhouse the night before standing outside his truck.

"What do you want?" Ghost asked without lowering his window.

"We need to talk," the man said.

Options raced through Ghost's mind. Did this man know who he was? Where he'd come from?

"Do I know you?" He still wasn't lowering the window. He wasn't going to give the man a chance to get the drop on him. No flicker of recognition, anger, or anything else crossed the man's face as he continued to meet Ghost's gaze.

"Get out of the truck," the stranger said.

Ghost wondered for a moment if he could start the truck and leave. Would he get away? A glance in the mirror next to where the man stood told him there was a large truck parked behind him blocking his exit from the driveway. How had they managed to get that there without him noticing? He looked back to the man and thought about pulling his pistol.

Would it do him any good? Before he had a chance to decide, the man lifted his own weapon, a semi-auto. In the darkness it was hard to tell the make for sure, but it looked like a 1911 style. Ghost knocked his phone off is lap as he lifted his hands so the man could see them, then used the heal of his boot to kick it under the seat. With any luck they wouldn't think to look there, and Malice would find it later.

Hell, with any luck, they'd question him and let him go and Malice wouldn't need to look. Ghost wasn't holding his breath on that one.

"Use one hand and open the door. Keep the other where I can see it." The stranger didn't point his pistol at Ghost. He didn't have to. He already had his weapon out, which meant he could have it aimed at Ghost and the trigger pulled in a fraction of the time it would take Ghost to pull his own and get it aimed.

Ghost did as he was told, lowering one hand only far enough to pop the latch on the door then lifting it back up where it could be seen. He used one knee to ease the door open. As tempting as it was to shove the door into the other man and knock him down, if the man had slipped up on him, logic told Ghost he wouldn't be alone. Ghost wouldn't be alone if it were him.

He waited while the stranger backed up then, keeping his hands in full view, pushed the door open, twisted in his seat and slid from the driver's seat to land on his feet. Hands still spread.

"I'm not sure what I've done wrong here." As far as he could tell, he would be best off to know nothing. Admit nothing. Even if they had proof. He would never give up the Souls. But if he was careful, he might be able to learn something.

"Move over there," the stranger used the pistol to motion toward the rear of the pickup, which also happened to be the street.

Ghost glanced in that direction, didn't see anyone, and moved a couple feet in the direction indicated.

"More."

Ghost took a couple more steps.

The stranger stepped into the open doorway and looked around the interior of the truck.

"Where's your phone?"

"Don't have it with me. I broke it earlier today and shipped it off to be replaced. Stupid fucking insurance companies." He hoped complaining about the company would make the story he'd just come up with more believable.

"I don't believe you. You've got to have some way to communicate, even if it's not a phone."

"All I've got is that tablet. It doesn't do much, but it will do email." He was glad he'd set up a free email program on it. It used the account he considered his public account. The one where his video streaming accounts were billed to. That would make it look like a main account if they looked that deep.

But Ghost had spent too much time working undercover to do something that obvious even his phone didn't access his main account through the apps. He did access it, but through the browser and made sure to use incognito browsing and log out every time. Even if they did find his phone, there was only a limited amount of information they would find on him and the Souls. That was if they could even break into it. Gizmo had set up the security on his phone and Ghost had yet to find anyone who could break Gizmo's encryption, except maybe Krissi. He hadn't asked but from the way those two worked together, he wouldn't put it past her.

Movement in front of him drew his attention back to the man with the gun. The stranger watched him with narrowed eyes a moment before reaching across the seat and snagging the tablet from the top of the console where Ghost had it sitting. He pulled the keys from the ignition and pocketed them, then tucked the tablet under his arm, hit the lock button on the door and closed it.

"Come on. Someone wants to talk to you." The stranger tilted his head to motion Ghost where he wanted him to go.

Ghost glanced in the direction then back at the man. Should he go? Should he fight? He still didn't see anyone else. He might get away. But he wouldn't learn anything that way. How much did he trust Malice to come find him?

"I'm not waiting all night. Get a move on or we'll end this right here." The stranger used the barrel of the pistol to motion Ghost toward Tank's house. While Ghost had several options run through his head, he dismissed them all and did what he was told, turning, and heading for the house he assumed belonged to the King's president.

⁂

Ghost rolled his neck, wincing as his ribs protested his moving. The last few hours hadn't been the most fun of his life, but he'd gotten through them. And better yet, he hadn't given up any information.

They'd brought him to the house, the man Ghost assumed was Tank, partly because at about five foot seven and somewhere near four hundred pounds, Ghost thought he looked like a tank, had asked why Ghost was watching him and who had sent him. Ghost acted as if he didn't know what they were talking about which hadn't gotten them anywhere and had only frustrated the Kings until Ghost got to see why they called themselves the Kings of Destruction, or at least he hoped that was why.

The man who had confronted him at the truck, who Ghost had learned was called Rooster, had taken him out to the garage, which was thankfully at least warmer than outside, though not as warm as in the house, and told him to sit in a straight backed metal and vinyl dining room chair that looked like a hold over from the seventies, setting in the middle of the room, as if it had been waiting for him. Ghost had already decided to go along, except for giving them information so he sat as he was told. Another flunky Rooster called Jonesy taped his hands together behind his back and his ankles to the legs of the chair. Ghost didn't fight or even try to talk them out of it, only watched like it was happening to someone else.

Once he was tied to the chair and couldn't stop them, they got a bit more aggressive with their questioning. Ghost didn't let that change his story.

"Who sent you?" Rooster demanded.

"No one sent me," Ghost had responded.

"Last chance," Tank had stood to one side of the room, leaning against a wall, totally relaxed as if they weren't threatening to hurt him. "Tell us who sent you and we'll let you go."

Like Ghost actually believed that. He knew they weren't going to just let him go. Rooster looked way too happy at the prospect of hurting someone.

"No one sent me."

"Then why are you here?"

"Why am I where? I was just sitting in my truck when this guy comes along with a gun, makes me get out and come here."

That's when the first blow had come. Rooster had hit him in the ribs with that first hit but he hadn't limited himself to just the ribs. He'd gone for the abdomen and the face.

No matter where, or how they'd hit him, he'd stuck to his story. After a couple hours they'd told him to think about it and left him in the garage, still taped to the chair while they'd gone inside, turning the lights out as they'd gone. He suspected Rooster had needed to ice his hands. And Ghost could use some ice himself, but the room was cool and that was almost as good.

Now as he stretched and tried to figure out how hurt he was, he spotted a thin line of light coming from below the big roll open door. That meant the sun was likely coming up. Malice would have missed him by now.

Had he found the truck? Had he located the phone?

A million other questions raced through Ghost's mind keeping him from thinking about the ache in his ribs or the dull throb of his face.

He had no doubt Malice would find him, the question was, how long would it take?

CHAPTER 31

Robyn was almost ready lay down for a short nap as she had the next two days off and didn't want to sleep them away, not when Ghost might call, when her phone rang. She frowned at the screen and the unknown number, debating whether or not she wanted to bother with what was probably a spam call.

But what if it wasn't? A voice in the back of her mind whispered. She still hadn't heard from Ghost and that didn't seem like him. Could he be ghosting her? Sure, but somehow, she didn't think so. Her gut told her something was wrong.

"Hello?" Robyn answered the phone and hoped it would be news, something. Even if it was Ghost telling her he was done. That had to be better than not knowing.

"Are you Robyn?" An unfamiliar male voice came across the line.

"I am. Can I ask who this is?"

"I know this is going to sound strange, but bear with me, please. My name is Malice. I'm a friend of Ghost's."

Her stomach did a summersault.

"I know who you are. He's mentioned you. Is he okay?" She fought to keep her voice from shaking. She was convinced something had kept him from being in touch.

"That's what I'm trying to find out. He's not with you?"

"No. I haven't seen him all day."

"When is the last time you saw him?"

"Actually laid eyes on him? About noon yesterday. He left here about six last night as far as I can tell. But he texted me last night. I haven't heard from him since about ten p.m." The uneasy feeling in her belly grew worse. This wasn't good. Something had happened to him, and his partner didn't know what.

"That's what I was afraid of. That's the last I can find of him right now. Do you know what he was doing last night? Did he say?"

"He said he was looking into a club here in town, give me a minute and I'll remember the name. He mentioned one guy and I asked my dad, he's a retired police officer. Dad said the guy's bad news. Tank, the guy's name was. Dad told me to stay as far away from Tank as I can because there's nothing having to do with him that isn't serious trouble." She paused to take a breath and when he didn't say anything right away, she continued, "Should we call the cops? Should I get more people looking for him?"

"Not yet. No one will take us seriously until he's been gone at least twenty-four hours. Not unless we have some kind of evidence of foul play."

Damn. He was right and she knew it.

"Wait a sec."

"What?"

"Where did you get my number and how did you know my name? Did Ghost give it to you?" She couldn't imagine that he had, not the way he'd talked about Malice but maybe?

"You were the last person he contacted from his phone. I found it in his truck." She thought there was something about that he wasn't telling her, but why would he tell her all of it?

"If you've got his phone isn't that enough sign of foul play?" She knew it wasn't, but had to ask, just in case he would tell her more.

"Unfortunately, no. The truck was locked, and the keys gone as if he'd walked away and fully planned to come back. I'll keep looking though. Will you let me know if you hear from him?"

"I will. At this number?"

"Please."

"And will you do the same? Have him call me when you find him or at least let me know he's okay?" She hoped she didn't sound as desperate as she felt. She tried to tell herself it was all right if he didn't want to see her anymore, as long as he was still out there. Still okay.

"I will. I'll make sure one of us contacts you once I've found him."

"Thank you." She wanted to say more, to say something, but what?

They rang off the call and she stared at the bed she had been getting ready to climb into. She couldn't sleep now. Not when she knew Ghost was missing and had been looking into some dangerous men. Not that she could do anything. At least nothing helpful.

She stared at her phone for a full minute before making up her mind and calling Dad.

"Hey, sweetheart, what are you up to today?"

"Trying to get stuff done on my day off, how about you?"

"Had coffee with the guys this morning. I've got a project in the shop I've been working on, and tonight is a retirement party for one of my old partners. But something tells me that's not what you're calling to hear about."

"I love knowing what you're doing, Dad, but you're right. I've got something else on my mind."

"Is it something I can help with?"

"I'm not sure. Well, honestly, probably not, but I needed someone to talk to and you're my favorite sounding board."

"Hit me with it. I'll see if there's anything we can do, sweetheart."

"So, I've been seeing this guy..." she told him about Ghost and why she'd asked about Tank before. Then explained that Ghost had disappeared in the middle of the night and what little Malice had told her over the phone. He asked a few questions, and she told him everything she knew, which even she had to admit, wasn't much.

"I don't know that there's anything we can do but let me make a few calls. I'll see if I can learn anything then call you back. Hold tight, sweetheart."

Her heart warmed at the endearment Dad had always called her. It wasn't the same as Ghost's sunshine, but it made her feel similar, for different reasons. She just hoped she'd get to hear him call her sunshine again.

"All right. I know my going out and looking will only make things harder, but I don't know how long I can just sit here."

"Do chores. It's something you can do mostly on auto pilot but will keep you busy. I'll try to get back to you before you're through with your weekly cleaning."

Ghost didn't know how long he'd been sitting taped to the chair. Long enough that the sun had come up and the garage was almost warm. He'd sagged against his bonds and slept when he could, at least until his screaming shoulders and throbbing ribs wouldn't let him rest any longer. And still no one had returned.

There had been muffled sounds of traffic on the street, but he couldn't tell if the muffled sounds were because the garage was that well insulated, he doubted it because of the temperature, or because of the snow outside.

Then again, he wasn't hearing any sound from inside the house, so maybe it was at least partly insulation.

Ghost wondered if Malice had found the truck yet. Had he found the phone? Would he contact Lurch when he couldn't find Ghost? How long would he wait before doing that? Ghost could only hope it wasn't days. Or more than a few hours. Hopefully soon.

He rolled his shoulders as much as the tape on his arms would allow, then flexed as much as the bruises and stiff muscles would let him. Getting out of here would be painful. And as much as he wanted to be cut loose, he wasn't looking forward to that part. He felt around the back of the chair as he flexed, trying to find a sharp spot or a rough spot, anything to rub the tape against and maybe cut or break it.

Nothing. Not even a loose screw that might help him. He bent his elbows, then straightened them, over and over. Ignoring the biting pain in his arms as he worked and worked the tape, trying to either make it not stick anymore or tear through it until he could free his hands, but it seemed no matter how hard he worked the binding, it wasn't loosening or working free. He wondered if maybe they had managed to reinforce the tape somehow, but how?

He was still trying to work himself free when he heard shouting somewhere nearby. He didn't think it was in the house, but he couldn't be sure. Then there was a loud crash. He froze. There was no way to be certain, but he thought that was the front door being knocked in.

Ghost's heart thundered in his ears. Did that mean they were coming to get him or was it a coincidence? He didn't believe in coincidences, whether they were looking for him or not. They were going to find him. He just had to wait. It wouldn't be long now. That didn't stop him from trying to work himself free.

Noise continued as he focused on trying to loosen his hands, ignoring the pain that shot through him every time he moved. He heard a door open behind him.

"I got someone in the garage," a voice he didn't recognize said. "Have emergency services ready as soon as we clear the house. This guy's going to need them." There was some squawking over a radio, but Ghost was too focused on what he was doing to try to make it out. A body in armor stepped into his line of sight. It took Ghost seconds to realize it was a police officer in S.W.A.T. gear.

"What's your name, sir?"

"Ghost," he said automatically.

"Sir, I need your legal name."

"Sorry." Ghost shook his head, trying to clear it. "Alex Hardy." Just saying the name felt weird. He hadn't used it in so long he didn't even feel like it was his name anymore.

"I got him. Send the EMT's in." The man moved around behind him and in seconds his hands came free. It took him a moment to pull his arms around in front. The throbbing in his shoulders and ribs wouldn't let him move them like he wanted, but he was glad he was able to pull them forward.

In what seemed like seconds, he had two people in front of him, they'd brought a gurney and as much as he hated it, he knew he was going to leave here on that thing. They asked him what seemed like a million questions.

Name, did he know what day it was, did he know where he was? Ghost answered them all, letting them know that while he was sure he looked like shit, he was fairly certain he didn't have a brain injury.

It took a few minutes, but they got him cut loose, evaluated, on the gurney and headed out of the house. On the sidewalk in front of the house he spotted Malice.

"You look like shit, you all right?" his buddy asked.

"I'll be okay. They're going to take me in. See you there?"

"I'll meet you there. Want me to call your girl? She's worried about you."

Fuck. He knew he'd forgotten something. Not because she didn't matter, but because he'd pushed her out of his mind so he wouldn't accidentally say something and send these asshats after her.

"Yeah, call her. Let her know you found me and where they're taking me." He let his head fall back against the gurney. She was safe. He wasn't seriously hurt. Yeah, he'd be in pain for a few weeks, but that was far better than the alternative.

CHAPTER 33

Robyn was getting frantic. Dad had called back, but he hadn't been able to tell her anything more. She'd finished with the house and then wandered around looking for something to keep herself busy. Anything.

Malice would call her if there was news or Ghost would call her himself. She just had to wait. She hated waiting. In a desperate drive for some thing to do to keep from mindlessly pacing through the house and driving herself nuts with worry, she pulled everything from the linen closet, sorted, refolded it all and was working on putting it away neatly when her phone rang.

She pounced on it before the first ring completed. The number was the same one Malice called from earlier.

"Did you find him?" She didn't even bother with a greeting.

"We did. He's a little beat up, but he's talking. I don't think he's hurt too bad but they're taking him to the hospital to get checked out."

Her heart seemed to skip a beat when he said Ghost had been found. Then her stomach sank when she heard he was being taken to the hospital. She hesitated to ask but she had to. The words wouldn't come out the first try. She had to swallow and try again.

"Does he want me there?"

"I'm sure he does. He asked me to call you and let you know where they're taking him. I want to warn you though, he's pretty beat up. I don't think it's anything permanent, but it looks like they beat on him for a while."

"All right. I think I can handle that." She didn't bother to try to keep her voice from shaking. Her knees shook and she didn't try to stop herself from sinking to her knees then to sit on her butt in the middle of the hall where she'd been putting things into the closet.

"You don't need to rush over there, it will be a few minutes before they get him there, do the initial eval and are willing to let people back to see him. Are you okay to drive?"

"I think so."

"No. Don't try it. Give me your address. I'll come pick you up. Ghost will kill me if I let you drive yourself and you end up in an accident."

She gave him her address; he told her he'd be there in a few minutes, and they disconnected. She sat blinking for she didn't know how long then realized she needed to get ready. She left everything where it lay and went to dress to go out. She didn't care what Malice said about not letting anyone back to see him. She needed to be there. She needed to know he was all right.

By the time she'd dressed and put on her shoes, a full sized pickup had pulled up outside her house. When she heard the engine shut off, she didn't wait for him to come to the door. Instead, she stepped outside and met him beside the truck.

"Malice?" she asked at the same time he spoke.

"Robyn?"

She nodded and didn't wait for him to say anything else before going to the passenger door. He hit the button to unlock it and she climbed inside. Once he'd gotten back inside and they were on the road she couldn't keep herself from asking.

"Do you know anything more? How hurt is he?"

"I haven't heard. I saw him for just a few minutes as they brought him out and put him in the ambulance."

Her stomach dropped. He'd needed an ambulance.

"Do you know what happened?"

"I don't. I only have a little information. After I talked to you, I contacted our employers, they made a few calls and the next thing I know I was given an address and told to meet the police there."

"And they brought him out hurt." She looked down at her hands. They were folded together in her lap, knuckles white as she tried to hold it together. "I don't know if it helped, but I called my dad and told him what I knew. Asked him to see if there was anything he could do. He'd a retired Stark County Sheriff's Deputy and has friends still in the department. I had asked him about Tank for Ghost, so I told Dad that Ghost was missing and that he'd been looking into Tank and his club." She looked up and out the window beside her. The town she'd lived in nearly all her life sped past, but she didn't register its passing or even where they were. "Thanks for coming to get me. You're right. I shouldn't be driving."

"You sure you're up for this? I can take you back to the house if you'd like."

She turned and stared at him a moment trying to see if he was serious. There was no way she would be going home without making sure Ghost was okay. Hell, if she had her way, he would be coming home with her when she they cut him loose.

She wondered how long he'd have to stay and how hard she'd have to fight Malice to get Ghost where she wanted him. Somehow, she didn't think Ghost was one she'd have to fight about it.

CHAPTER 34

By the time the doctors and nurses had finished poking and prodding him and he'd answered all the questions from the police, Ghost felt like they'd drawn half his blood and scanned his entire body. He knew it had only been x-rays and a head CT looking for bleeding because of how beat up he was. But at least they'd given him something for the pain.

He'd refused the narcotics they'd wanted to give him. He didn't want them messing with his head. He needed to talk to Malice and give a report to Lurch, and maybe Gizmo, but more than either of those, he wanted to see Robyn.

It was foolish, and not as important as sharing what he knew about Tank and the Kings, but all he wanted was to lay down beside her and sleep for a while.

"You seem to have no lasting injuries, Mr. Hardy. But I suggest you take it easy for a few weeks. You have four ribs that are bruised on your left side, the obvious on your face and I'm sure none of that feels good. Manage your pain with Tylenol and intermittent ice packs to help with the swelling." The doctor droned on a little while longer then told him they would be discharging him, and the nurse would be bringing him the paperwork. "There are a couple people in the waiting room for you, would you like me to let them come back so they can help you get ready to leave?"

"Please." Ghost let his head fall back against the bed as the doctor left the room. Two? Was Robyn here too? There hadn't been time for anyone else to get here, either from Wyoming or Arizona, though it seemed like he'd been here for a couple days, it was probably only a couple of hours.

More than once he wished he had his phone, at least then he could be communicating with people while he waited.

"You sure know how to get a girl's attention, don't you?"

Ghost almost didn't open his eyes at Malice's voice, but the doctor had said two people and Ghost hoped Robyn was with him. He opened his eyes to see Robyn standing beside the bed, her hands folded together in front of her, knuckles white.

"Hey, sunshine. Glad to see you." He winced as he'd tried to smile at her, and it hurt. Instead, he reached the hand closest to her and took her hand, distracting her from whatever she'd been doing with them. With his other hand, he flipped off Malice.

"You look like it hurts." Robyn blinked back the tears that pooled in her eyes before they had a chance to fall.

He hated that she fought so hard to be strong for him. He didn't want that for her. He wanted to be the one to be strong, to take care of her, to protect her.

The fierce need to protect her surprised him, he'd never felt anything quite like it, not for someone he had been seeing so short a time. Usually, he only felt so protective of his brothers.

He rubbed his thumb over the back of hers.

"It's sore but it's not too bad. Nothing permanent and they said they'll be letting me go soon."

"They're not admitting you?" That was from Malice.

"Nope. No need according to the doc. I'll be sore. I've got bruised ribs, and a few stitches in my face but no concussion or internal bleeding."

"That's good. What kind of meds do they have you on? Can you drive?"

"Nothing mind altering. I refused those. Said to take Tylenol and ice once this wears off. So, can I drive? Technically I'm sure I could. But I'd prefer not to. Not if I can help it."

Malice bobbed his head a couple times but didn't say anything, not right away.

"So how do we want to do this? What are you going to do when they cut you lose?" Malice asked after a moment.

"I want to lay down and sleep. Let myself heal for a while before I have to do anything. I slept off and on but not well. They had me tied to a chair so I'm pretty sure every muscle in my body hurts."

"I want you to come home with me," Robyn spoke up, her hand squeezed his gently. As if she was afraid that she would hurt him of she squeezed too hard.

"I'd like that."

"I'm okay with it but I need some help first. We need to pick up your truck and I can't do that alone."

"I can drive it," Robyn said.

Ghost looked up to find her face had turned red.

"I mean if that's okay with you." She glanced at Malice then looked back to him.

"Then let me make a suggestion," Malice said. "When they cut you loose, we all load up in my truck. Then we go get your truck. I talked the cops at the scene out of your keys, since they found them on a work bench near where they found you. Robyn can take it back to her place. I'll swing by the motel and pick up anything you might need then I'll take you back to her place. That will keep us from having to move you too much from one vehicle to another and get whatever you need for the next couple days."

"Sounds like a plan. We just need them let me out of here." He met Malice's gaze for a moment, knowing that moving him between vehicles wasn't why Malice had suggested they do things that way. He'd done it so the two of them would have a chance to talk. So, Ghost could report what had happened, probably both to him and to Lurch, then he could go recover, without it seeming odd to Robyn.

"You got my phone?" he asked Malice. He was tired of being out of touch and needed something other than how bad he hurt to occupy his mind.

&

"I didn't know if we wanted your girl to know I've got a second set of keys to you truck, but I also didn't want to leave keys with the Kings. Talking the cops out of yours seemed like the best option. I wasn't so lucky with your pistol. The cops are keeping it for a while. At least until they run it through NIST and do some testing. Now tell me what happened," Malice said after they dropped Robyn off at his truck and watched her drive away.

Ghost gave him a run down of everything that had happened and what he'd heard the Kings say. From what they'd let him overhear, he didn't think they'd planned to let him go. They'd said way too much to let him walk away. He was a liability.

"Did you tell all this to the police when they questioned you?"

"All but about the Souls. We do our best to stay off the radar to law enforcement."

Malice nodded, staying quiet for a moment as he navigated traffic. "What do you want me to tell Lurch?"

"Everything. I'll reach out to him and talk to him myself. Are you going to load up my things or do I need to go do it?" He wasn't sure if the not moving from one vehicle to another was to keep Robyn from questioning why she didn't just take him home with her or not.

"I'll get it. You call Lurch. Anything specific you want or just everything?"

"You can load it all up if you want. I want to keep the room though, it's cheaper with the weekly rate anyway and I may be back sooner rather than later." He knew from experience, women got tired of him real quick. Ghost had no illusions. He was a pain in the ass, and he knew it. He was mostly happy with who he was though, so he didn't see any reason to change.

They pulled into the parking lot at the motel, Malice went inside, and Ghost dialed Lurch. Time to make his official report. At least as much as he would be making for a few days.

"This is Lurch."

"Hey prez, how's it hanging?" He knew there were better ways to greet the president of the club, but no one expected it of him. He'd worked hard to set up his reputation as a pain in the ass and more than a little lacking in respect. He got away with it for several reasons, not in the least was he was good enough at what he did to let the attitude problems slide.

"Glad to hear they found you."

"You knew they found me. Malice would have told you that before I made it to the hospital."

Lurch chuckled on the other end of the line, letting Ghost know he was right. "What's the damage?"

"Physically or operationally?"

"Both, but since you're calling and you don't sound high, I'm going to assume the physical isn't too bad, so let's start with the operational."

"They knew I came from the ranch, and that we're the Souls. From what they said, the order to harass us came from their parent chapter in Billings, but it gets a little hazy from there. One said something about orders coming from outside the club, another wasn't happy about that. There was some fighting among them, but I didn't get all of it."

"Sounds like they let you hear a lot."

"Agreed. I don't think they planned to let me live. Don't know if it was you or Gizmo who found me and sent the local LEOs in, but thanks either way."

"Malice called but you know me, I can barely get my phone to do what I need it to. I set Giz on your trail. He found you in no time. It took a little longer to get through the red tape to get you out of there, but I'm glad we did. Now tell me what else you have on these guys."

Ghost spent a few minutes filling his chapter president in on everything they'd learned about the Kings since they'd gotten to Dickenson, including what Robyn's father had told them and all the rest of the research he'd managed to find. He knew he'd likely have to put it all in writing and probably repeat it to either Gizmo or Krissi, but he was okay with that. He was sitting still and not hurting too bad, at the moment, so it was something to fill the time.

"Is that all?" Lurch asked after Ghost had given him everything he could remember.

"I think so. If I remember more, I'll let you know."

"Good. Now fill me in on the physical damage."

Ghost did as he asked, outlining his injuries in nearly the same clinical manner the doctor had before he'd let him leave.

"What are your plans from here?" Lurch asked when he'd finished.

"I'm not entirely sure. We still need to confront Tank. Make sure they stop harassing our women. But I need a couple days to heal before I can be in on that, and I don't think I can make that drive right now. The idea of even sitting in a vibrating truck for an hour, much less five, sets my teeth on edge. I haven't talked to Malice about the plan yet, but I'm going to take a couple days to recover. I'll see if we can't come up with something he can do to keep with forward progress, without risking him ending up like me."

"Sounds good. Keep me appraised of what's going on up there and the plans. I can send someone else up to help if I need to, but it will stretch us thin here."

"No. Don't do that. Not yet. Give us some time. I'll let you know if we need help."

"Do that, and don't go all cowboy on me. I know you sniper teams are used to being on your own in some rough situations, but you're not now. There is backup. Use it if you need to."

"Yes, sir." Ghost let his tone show he wasn't entirely serious with that response, hoping Lurch would take it in the way he meant it.

"Fuck you. Keep that shit for the officers."

"But you are an officer now, prez. Or did that not occur to you?"

"Damn it. I hadn't thought about that. But you're an officer too, just not as high in rank. And if you start saluting me, I'll put you on every shit duty I can think of for a year."

Ghost started to laugh, then stopped and winced. "Ouch. Don't make me laugh. It hurts."

"Serves you right. You started this." Lurch didn't sound the least bit repentant. "Ok, you go rest, get better. We need you to wrap this up and get back down here."

"Oh." He decided to ask this last question on impulse, fully aware he'd probably regret it. But Malice knew about Robyn, and he'd never live it down with him, what was the harm in adding Lurch to that list? "What are the chances I might could get some kind of housing away from the bunkhouse?" Maybe he was rushing this, but he hated the idea of leaving Robyn here. Especially after she spent a few days with his truck outside her place, letting the Kings know she was involved with him.

"I'm not sure. I'll have to check with Tuck and see what's available. You getting too good to bunk with the men?"

"Nah, I'm just thinking my girl might not want to live like that."

"You have a girl? One you're considering bringing back with you?" The shock was clear in Lurch's voice.

Ghost had known it would be surprising but hadn't expected that level of surprise.

"I haven't talked to her about it yet. I wanted to see if getting a place outside of the bunkhouse was possible first."

"I'll see what we've got and let you know."

"Thanks."

Malice came out of Ghost's room, his rucksack swung over one shoulder. Ghost rang off with Lurch and waited for Malice to take him to Robyn's. The idea of a soft bed with her warm body beside him sounded heavenly.

CHAPTER 35

Robyn pulled Ghost's truck up in front of her house and sat there a moment. They would be at least a few minutes behind her. She let herself calm down.

Ghost was hurt, yes. But it wasn't as it could have been. It wasn't as bad as she'd feared. In a few days or a few weeks, he would be fine. As good as if this had never happened. And where would she be? She wasn't going to think about that right now. That wasn't what mattered right now. Taking care of Ghost did. She took a deep breath, got out of the truck, and went inside to get busy. She'd left a mess and needed to get it cleaned up, so she didn't have to worry about it while Ghost was here.

It took her longer than she'd hoped, but she got everything picked up and put away before the guys pulled up, though not by much. She was standing in the kitchen, staring into the open refrigerator, wondering what to make for dinner when a knock sounded on her front door. That had to be them.

She spotted Malice's truck on the curb behind Ghost's as she made her way to the door to let them in. She found Ghost standing on the top step, Malice a couple steps behind him a camo backpack with a bunch of thin straps hanging off all over, slung over one shoulder.

"Come on in, get off your feet. You want to have a seat in the living room for a while or go lay down?"

"I've been laying in that hospital bed for the last few hours. Before that I was taped to a dining room chair for at least twelve hours. I want to sit some where soft and comfortable for a little while, then go lay down and try to get a little sleep."

"Not a problem." She ushered them both into the living room where she offered to help Ghost sit but he waved her away and eased himself onto the sofa. She turned to Malice. "Have a seat." She motioned to a couple other chairs in the room.

"Where do you want this?" Malice asked, swinging the backpack off his shoulder.

"In the bedroom would—"

"Here," Ghost interrupted her. "My clothes are in it, but there are a couple of other things I want out first. I'll take it in the bedroom later."

"Then let's put it here." Robyn pointed to a spot at the end of the sofa. She had no intention of letting Ghost carry it into the other room. She'd wait until he was resting then take it herself.

"When is the last time you ate?" she asked Ghost. "I'm sure if you were stuck in a chair, they didn't feed you."

"No, they didn't, and I'm hungry what I really want is you sitting here beside me, not cooking." Ghost patted the seat beside him.

"But you need to eat." She glanced toward the kitchen and wondered what she had that she could put in the oven and let cook while she spent the time with him like he wanted.

"I'm sure they have pizza places that deliver here," Malice said from the chair beside the sofa. "Let me just order delivery." He pulled his phone from his pocket. "Do you have a favorite place?" he asked Robyn.

She gave him the name of a local pizza place that delivered here, though she didn't order from them often. "What about toppings?"

"Pepperoni good for everyone?" Malice asked.

"Fine by me. You know that," Ghost said.

"That's fine." She knew it would be easier, and they would be more likely to get the right pizza if the order was simple.

"Do we need drinks?" Malice asked as he tapped something out on his screen.

"I've got pop, milk, water, and tea. There might be a beer or two in there, I'll have to check."

"That's fine," Malice said, then paused and looked at Ghost, "unless you want something else?"

Ghost gave his head a small shake then let his head drop back against the back of the sofa, as if it was heavy and he was tired of holding it up. She had no doubt he was tired. He'd said he hadn't had much sleep since he'd been taken. She knew how that was because she hadn't either. He had gotten up a short while before she had the night before and she hadn't been able to rest while he was missing.

Ghost let out a big yawn, which made her yawn too.

"Another hour, some food in your belly, and we can get some sleep." Robyn sat beside him, not wanting to get too close and hurt any of the myriad of bruises still blooming on his face and she was sure his torso, she tried to be there to comfort him, though she didn't know how well she was doing. If it were her, she thought, she'd be content just to have him there, beside her, but Robyn had a hard time silencing the voice in the back of her head that told her she should be doing something. She should be helping in some tangible way. Ghost took her hand and tugged her closer.

"I don't want to hurt you."

"I'll let you know if it hurts, sunshine. Right now, I want you close to me." He didn't open his eyes or lift his head, just tightened his fingers in hers and tugged her closer.

"All right." She scooted closer then looked at Malice. "I take it you work the same ranch in Wyoming Ghost does?"

"I do. But I'm new there. I just started a couple weeks ago."

She frowned. "That new, and they sent you up here already?" She wondered if he was that bad at ranching or if he had some specialized skill to use up here.

"Yes, ma'am. I knew Ghost a long time ago and well, he can be a little difficult to work with. I guess they decided I'd known him long enough to not be put off by his prickly attitude."

"I'll show you prickly if you don't shut the fuck up," Ghost said, still without picking up his head or opening his eyes.

"I'm sorry. I didn't mean to disturb your rest. I'll be quiet so you can sleep."

"You're not disturbing me, sunshine. But that asshole over there is going to let his mouth get him in trouble."

She stared at Malice, wondering how he would take the threat.

Malice shook his head and rolled his eyes. "You're proving my point, old man. Prickly, grouchy, the same thing really."

Movement from Ghost made her turn and look at him, to find he was flipping the other man off, his head still resting against the back of the sofa, eyes still closed. Robyn looked back at Malice and found him grinning.

"He's not too hurt if he's willing to give me shit."

"I told you I'm not that hurt. I'm sore and I'm tired."

"And hungry," Malice reminded him. "And let's not forget your bruised ribs. Those will be sore as you call it, for a few weeks, not just a couple days."

"You're just aching for me to show you how not hurt I am, aren't you?"

The threat in Ghost's tone sounded real to Robyn, but from Malice's reaction, it wasn't as dire as it sounded. Malice grinned at her.

"If you've only been with the ranch for a little while, what were you doing before that?" Robyn didn't want to be a bad host, so she tried to keep Malice engaged in small talk.

"I was tending bar in Billings when that one got a hold of me." He nodded his head toward Ghost.

"Tending bar?" Somehow that didn't fit. She didn't know Malice well or at all really but tending bar just seemed off.

Malice gave a half shrug. "It's the off season for construction and I hadn't found anything else since I separated."

"From your wife? I'm so sorry."

Malice shook his head. "From the Marines."

"That's where I knew him from, sunshine. Malice was my spotter when I was with the Marines." Ghost's voice sounded a little better, and he wasn't so tense as he sat beside her.

Robyn frowned. Spotter? She didn't know a lot about the military but what kind of job used a spotter? She looked back and forth between the two men.

"How long have you known each other?"

"What's it been? Eight, nine years?" Malice asked.

"Ten."

She was quiet for a few seconds. Ghost hadn't mentioned anything about the military had he? Something niggled in the back of her mind, so maybe he had, but what branch? The big camo bag Malice had carried in caught her attention. It was larger than most backpacks. She'd seen a lot of camo during hunting season, and some in the off seasons. This wasn't the standard hunting camo pattern, what was that called? Mossy Oak her dad had called it. This was a military camo pattern. She'd never learned to differentiate the different patterns and tell what branch it belonged to, but this wasn't the tree-looking stuff that was available in any hunting store.

"What's got your mind spinning so fast, sunshine?" Ghost's voice drew her back to the present.

"I know you said something about the military before, but I can't remember which branch. How long ago did you get out?"

He watched her a moment, his confusion clear on his face. "I'm a marine, sunshine. You were playing with my tat yesterday. What did you think it meant?"

"The lightning bolt S's? I didn't know that had to do with the military?" She frowned as she tried to remember if she'd ever seen the symbol before. She didn't think so, but she couldn't be sure. She had never paid much attention to military metals or badges.

"Lightning bolts?" Ghost sounded confused.

"They do kind of look like lightning. Especially if you've seen those wizard school movies. They look like the scar on the kid's head," Malice said.

She turned and looked at him.

"That's what they look like. I couldn't place it, but maybe that's why I thought lightning."

Ghost sighed beside her but didn't say anything. She was about to ask what the twin S's meant when the doorbell rang. She released Ghost's hand and stood.

"That's probably the pizza. I'll get it if you don't mind?" Malice said, already standing.

"Go ahead. I'll grab plates and drinks then we can eat in here.

"No." Ghost sat up. "Let's eat in the kitchen."

"Let me help you up." Robyn hovered nearby in case he had trouble getting up.

"No. I can do it. Go get things ready. It will take me a minute, but I can do it." His tone was a little grumpy, and she could see why. He must feel helpless, she would. She watched him a moment then went ahead into the kitchen to gather stuff so they could eat.

CHAPTER 36

"You were right. I needed to eat before going to bed. I wouldn't have slept well on an empty stomach. Thank you for ordering dinner." Ghost sat in one of the two chairs at the tiny table in Robyn's kitchen. He met Malice's gaze. "But now that we're done eating, I need to get some rest. I'm going to get Robyn to come to bed with me, so you need to leave."

"Ghost!" Robyn's voice was incredulous. As if she couldn't believe he'd said that. He wondered for a split second which part had surprised her, that he wanted her to come to bed with him or that he'd told Malice to leave so they could.

"I don't want to leave you here defenseless," Malice said after a moment. "You had your pistol on you, right? They didn't find it in the house that I know of. They did find some weapons, but I don't think yours was one of them, and even if they did, it's in evidence. What if they see your truck on the street and come back after you?"

"We aren't defenseless." Robyn's words made them both turn to look at her. "What? I told you my dad was a cop. He taught me to shoot when I was younger and made sure I have a weapon, just in case."

"What kind of weapon?"

"It's a pistol. A .45." She looked defensive. Ghost didn't want her to feel like she needed to defend herself to him.

"Good. Where is it? Can I see it?" He needed to be sure it was something he could count on. Not something that had never been cleaned or was gummed up with too much oil and dust.

"It's in the nightstand beside the bed. Let me go get it." She stood and went into the bedroom.

"I'm still not comfortable leaving you here alone. Not with your truck out there advertising where you are," Malice said, keeping his voice low.

"So, you take that truck and leave me the new one. It's mine anyway. The only reason I was using that one was because I was only out there in the dark. I was hoping they wouldn't recognize it."

"That was a fail," Malice said, deadpan.

"Watch it, or you'll be hurting more than I am. And don't think I'm not in good enough shape to do it to you. Remember what I always told you. You have to sleep sometime."

Malice scowled, but didn't say anything more as Robyn came back into the room and laid a 1911 cutdown on the table in front of Ghost.

Ghost picked it up, looked it over, popped the magazine loose to make sure it was loaded, then slid the magazine home and pulled back the slide enough so he could see the round in the chamber.

"This is a nice little Ruger." He flexed his hand around the grip. It was a little smaller than he preferred, but he could make it work. "Here, you can put it back." He set it on the table in front of her, careful that he kept the muzzle pointed away from anyone. She picked up and walked away.

"It looks good, but will it be enough?"

"I'm not sure. Give me your pistol and take another one out of the safe in the truck. There's a key to it on the ring."

"There's a safe in the truck?" Malice stared at him brows lifted.

"Under the rear seat." Ghost waved his fingers at Malice in a hand it over motion.

Malice gave him an unhappy look but reached behind his back and pulled out his pistol and holster. He'd just pulled the whole thing from his belt and handed it to Ghost. Ghost didn't bother to go through the inspection steps he'd done with Robyn's. He'd seen Malice handle it enough over the last week, he knew it was well cared for and loaded.

"Where are the keys to the truck, sunshine? Malice is going to trade vehicles with us," Ghost said when Robyn came back into the kitchen. "That way he won't have to worry about those assholes coming back for me. Or at least he won't have to worry so much." Ghost shot Malice a mocking grin.

"Oh. What did I do with them when I came in?" She looked confused for a moment then her face cleared. "I hung them on the hook like I do my keys when I come in." She took Malice down the short hall to give him the keys. Ghost saw her covering a yawn as they both came back into the kitchen.

Ghost pushed himself out of the chair, fighting back the wince as the movement pulled at his ribs, shooting a sharp pain through them.

"All right. We've eaten, we're protected." He picked up Malice's pistol from the table and kept moving toward the front of the house, ushering Malice back in the direction he'd just come from. "It's time for you to go so we can get some rest."

"Ghost. Don't be rude," Robyn protested.

"I'm not being rude. I'm being honest. It's been nearly twenty-four hours since you slept, or since I slept comfortably. We're both exhausted. Malice understands." He continued to usher Malice toward the door. "If you need me, you can call. Don't need me for at least twelve hours. Unless it's urgent, call Lurch." Ghost resisted the urge to shove Malice out the door and slam it. Instead, he waited, almost patiently, while Malice and Robyn exchanged niceties then he let Malice out, closed and locked the door behind him. Once his partner was gone, he turned, leaned against the door, and let out a sigh, though a small one because deep breaths hurt.

"I thought he would never leave."

"Because you want to go to sleep?" Robyn's tone said she didn't believe him.

"Because I want a hot shower, if you don't mind, then to lay down beside you and get some sleep. I'd kill to say I had more fun things in mind, but in all honesty, I just want to get clean and hold onto you while I rest."

She stared at him a moment, as if trying to gauge the truth of his words, then sighed.

"Come on. Let's get you showered so we can get some sleep."

CHAPTER 37

By the time she'd gotten him into the shower, Robyn had to admit to herself she needed to see how bad his injuries were. Was there a better way to do it than to climb into the shower with him? Probably. But none of them were so tempting. Besides, the door was already locked, she'd seen the second pistol, this one in a holster, sitting on top of the nightstand. She wasn't worried about their safety, not in that way. But she was grimy from spending the morning cleaning. She might not be as in need of the shower as he was, but she could use one too. Might as well kill two birds with one stone. She stripped off then opened the door and stepped into the steam.

"You're going to hurt yourself that way. Here, give it to me." She held out one hand for the cloth he was using to soap up with, and waited until he handed it over. She carefully soaped him up, being extra careful of the bruises still blooming over the ribs on his left side, as well as anywhere else the skin looked even a little discolored. "Tell me what these mean," she said as she ran one finger over the tattoo they'd talked about earlier.

"You sure you want to know?"

She didn't answer, just stopped what she was doing and stared at him until he gave in.

"SS for scout sniper."

"You were a sniper. I can see why you might not want to share that. Some people are fascinated by the idea and ask a billion questions and for way too much detail."

He was silent for a moment. "You've seen people do that?"

"Not to a sniper," she said with a shrug. "But I once dated a guy who did it to my dad. It only took the one date for me to realize he was just looking for a way to get closer to a police officer and ask creepy morbid questions. There was no second date."

"I'm glad to hear it. And doubly glad you don't have any of those questions. I don't want you to feel like I'm hiding things from you, but there are some things I can't or won't talk about. Most of my time in the Marines falls under that, but not all."

"I'll let you know if you ever make me feel like you're hiding things. There was a lot Dad never talked about. He did his best to keep work at work and not bring it home. I understand the need to do that, especially with some jobs." She met his gaze trying to let him know she was serious.

"I don't know how I got so lucky." He tugged her close and dropped a soft kiss on her lips before pulling away. "Come on, let's finish up in here. I'm dead on my feet."

Robyn did her best not to let the shudder that wanted to race through her go at his words. She knew it was just an expression, but they had come way too close to just that for her comfort. How had she fallen so fast for anyone much less a stranger?

They finished in the shower, and she helped him towel off, not because he couldn't but because it would hurt him less if she did.

"You go on in and lay down. I've got a couple more things I've got to do in here, but I'll be in in just a minute." She let him go ahead then took care of her post shower routine, shy of drying her hair. She did brush it out and pull it back into a braid so it wouldn't be everywhere in the morning, then brushed her teeth and washed her face before going to join Ghost.

She found him lying on his back to one side of the bed, staring up at the ceiling.

"Are you comfortable?" she asked, thinking he didn't look ready to sleep.

"Not really. I like to lay on my left side but that's out for a while. I might sleep on my back, but I think it will be better on my other side. But I hate lying on that side unless there's a reason."

"And the pain of lying on the other side isn't a good enough reason?"

"It is. I won't be lying on that side for a while. But I can think of something that will make it easier." He used his foot to roll him onto his right side, she didn't miss the grimace he fought to hide. He patted the bed in front of him. "Come curl up with me. I'll sleep better if you're here with me."

"I'm coming, just let me grab a night shirt." She moved to the closet where she kept them hung up.

"Forget the shirt. I want to feel your skin against mine."

Robyn turned and gave him an assessing look. "Are you sure you won't take that as an invitation to do something you really shouldn't be?"

"Sunshine, I'd be dead if I didn't want to take you up on that unspoken invitation, but as much as I want to, it would hurt too much right now. Come on to bed and let's get some sleep." He patted the bed again. She narrowed her eyes at him, not sure if she should trust him. Hell, what if he wanted something more fun than sleep? Maybe she could find a way to give him what he wanted without letting it hurt him. She turned off the lights and joined him in bed, sighing as he wrapped his arm around her middle and tugged her tight against him. It only took a few moments for his breathing to even out as he drifted off to sleep. Robyn couldn't help the soft smile of contentment that curved her own lips as she drifted off to sleep herself.

CHAPTER 38

His entire body throbbing woke Ghost. It only took him a moment to remember where he was and what had happened. The softy body curled against him, softly snoring, didn't hurt with that. It took him a moment to ease himself away from her and out of bed. He needed to use the restroom rather badly.

When he was done in the bathroom he glanced at the clock. 10:47 p.m. They'd been asleep for a few hours, but nowhere near long enough to be rested. He eased into the kitchen for a drink, taking his phone with him and trying not to wake Robyn. He filled a glass and checked for messages while he drank the whole glass.

He was reading messages and information sent by Malice, Gizmo, and Lurch when Robyn came shuffling in.

"You all right?" she asked, her voice thick with sleep.

"Fine, just thirsty. Thought I'd check messages while I was up. I'll be back in just a minute, or you can come here and snuggle up to me while I finish."

That last suggestion he threw out as it occurred to him. He was surprised when she stepped close, wrapped her arms around his waist and laid her head against his chest, then just stood there.

"I woke up because I missed you." She rubbed her cheek against his skin. "How can you get used to sleeping beside someone so quickly?"

"I don't know. I've never spent more than one night with anyone." Ghost didn't know what made him say that. Not that it wasn't true, he just didn't usually share that much.

"How did they find you?" Her voice was soft, as if she didn't know if she should be asking. "Malice called to see if you were with me. I asked if we should call the police, he said they wouldn't start looking so soon, not without some kind of evidence. What kind of evidence did they have in order to find you so fast?"

Ghost let out a chuckle. He didn't even have to ask Malice or anyone else to know the answer to this one. It was something the club had started several years ago, after one of the brothers had been kidnapped by a rival club. It had taken them days to find him and by then they'd been too late to save his life. Determined that would never happen again, Lurch had ordered Gizmo to find a way to hide a GPS in something that wouldn't be suspected, or have any significant value so it wasn't removed or stolen.

"It was my watch."

As he'd expected her to do, she twisted around to see the cheap timekeeper.

"That? How would that let them find you? It doesn't even connect to a phone." She wasn't wrong.

He told her about the tiny locater beacon the Souls tech sergeant had managed to find to place in different items the men wore. And now that he thought about it, probably some of the women now too.

When he finished telling her about the locator devices, she frowned down at his watch then back up at him.

"If Malice knew about this, then why did he bother calling me? Why not just look up where you are?"

"Malice hasn't been with us long. And he's a ranch employee, not one of the Souls. He didn't know about it. Hell, I'm not sure if they even told him how they knew where I was. Though, he's not stupid. He probably put two and two together." He finished the water and set the glass aside. "Come on, sunshine. Let's go back to bed." He didn't have to ask twice. Robyn came willingly. Once they'd climbed back into bed, he was sound asleep less than ten minutes later.

⚘

The ringing of his cell phone woke him the next morning. He rolled over and reached for it, only to curl back on himself, holding his arm tight against his ribs.

"You all right?" Robyn's voice pierced the haze of pain clouding his brain.

"Yeah. See who's on the phone," he said between clenched teeth as he fought the urge to let loose a string of curses.

"It says Malice, want me to answer it?"

"Yeah, please." He was still focusing on breathing until the pain faded. He heard her answer his phone, but tuned her out as he tried to stop fighting the pain and instead relax and let it wash over him. He'd learned long ago that it passed faster if he didn't fight it.

"I tried to talk him out of it, but he insists he needs to talk to you." Robyn's voice cut into his attention. He took several breaths as deep as he dared then reached to take the phone.

"Talk to me," he said in way of a greeting.

"I went out to the truck to go pick up coffee and bring it to you. I know how you are about coffee, but when I got there, I found a note under the wiper."

"And?" There had to be more to this. Malice wouldn't have called for some flyer advertising a church service.

"It's for you, I'm sure. It says:

"'Sorry for the difficulty. We've cleaned house and would like to make amends.' Then there's a phone number. It's signed Kings of Destruction, New Regime."

"Hmm. Send me the number. I'll call in a while."

"Will do. I take it I should hold off on the coffee for a bit, I get the feeling I woke you."

"You did but bring it anyway. And something for breakfast." There was no way he would be going back to sleep with the pain that still throbbed through his ribs. "We'll see what this means, for us and the rest of the Souls."

"I take it we're getting up?" Robyn was sitting up beside him where she'd reached over him to get to the phone.

"I am, but you don't need to. You can go back to sleep if you're still tired." He didn't know how much he'd have to keep from her from the upcoming discussions, but she'd seen enough and taken not only his injuries, but his time in the Marines in stride. He would deal with the issues as they arose, and figure out how to deal when there was a problem.

"I might as well get up. I can help with whatever is going on, and if you need to me not around for things, I have chores I started to keep myself busy while they were looking for you. I can finish those." She scooted to the far edge and climbed out of bed with far more agility than he was feeling this morning.

He took as deep a breath as he dared and prepared himself to get up.

Once Ghost made it to his feet, he went into the living room to get his rucksack, only to have Robyn snatch it just before he laid his hands on it. Somehow, she'd found the time to put on an oversized sweatshirt and sweat pants. He couldn't help but wonder if she'd put on a bra, and if she'd let him find out.

"You are not carrying this. Not with those ribs." She hefted it onto one shoulder and carried it into the bedroom. She plopped it onto the bed. "There. Now you can pull out what you need without hurting yourself. Again. I'm going to go start coffee."

"Don't bother," he called after her, "Malice is bringing coffee and breakfast."

"He doesn't have to do that."

"Yes, he does. I told him to. It's the least he can do if he's going to come and intrude on our time, he can feed us. That way we don't have to waste time cooking or cleaning up after it. He's just compensating us for the time he's taking." Ghost glanced over to see if Robyn was buying his story.

She looked at him with narrowed eyes then shook her head and left as if she didn't know what to make of him and didn't have the patience for it right now anyway. So much for finding out if she was wearing a bra, at least not now. Ghost grinned to himself and opened his bag to dig out clothes for the day.

By the time he got a shirt and jeans on, Malice had arrived. He didn't bother with shoes as he padded into the kitchen. Coffee first. He'd worry about shoes before he left; if he needed to go out.

"What did you bring us?" he asked as he stepped into the room to find Malice standing at the counter unpacking several grocery bags.

"Coffee, of course. But I had no idea what you're girl likes for breakfast, so I hit a grocery store and picked up an assortment of donuts and bagels, as well as stuff to go on the bagels. I was looking for some kind of breakfast sandwich didn't see any ready to go."

Ghost glanced at Robyn and found her scanning the items Malice had spread along the counter.

"There are a few places that do breakfast in town, but I can work with this. I was missing bagels, but I've got the rest of the stuff for bagel sandwiches if you don't mind sausage instead of ham."

"Sausage is fine by me," Malice said.

"I prefer sausage but let me help you with it." Ghost stepped toward the counter.

"Think again." Robyn pulled a mug from the counter over her coffee pot and fixed him a cup of coffee. "Take this. Sit here or in the living room. Don't you have a call to make? I can handle putting together breakfast."

Ghost took the cup and scowled. He didn't like leaving her to wait on them.

"You're right. I do have a call to make. But Malice doesn't. He can help you." He shot the other man a look that said if Ghost found his assistance lacking, then there would be hell to pay.

"I'll help." Malice held his hands up as if proving he wasn't armed. "I don't mind helping, as long as you got everything covered there."

"I do."

"Then go on. I'll let you know when breakfast is ready." Robyn turned to the fridge and started pulling out ingredients.

Ghost took his coffee and went into the living room. It was probably the most privacy he would get for a while.

In the living room, he set his coffee on the table beside the chair and eased himself down. He'd never have admitted it, well maybe to Robyn but never to Malice, but he was pretty sore. He could only hope some of it worked out with movement, but he'd have to be careful how he moved because of those damned ribs.

Once he'd gotten comfortable, he pulled up the number Malice had sent him and hit dial.

"Hello?" A male voice came across the line. Not one of the men who'd been in the garage the day before, but that was all he could tell off hand.

"I had this number left on my truck last night."

A sigh echoed across the line. "You don't know me, but I want to offer you an apology. What happened to you never should have happened and we are making changes to our organization. I don't want trouble with you or any of your friends. What do we need to do to make this right?"

"First I need to know who I'm dealing with."

"My name is Cowboy. Cowboy Lovatt, but I don't think that's what you mean."

Ghost gave a chuckle then stopped halfway through as a sharp pain shot through his ribs. "It's a start. But I also want to meet you face to face. Have a sit-down discussion. In public. In a place of my choosing."

"You got it. When and where?"

That stumped him for just a minute. He didn't know Dickenson like Tucson, or even Gillette. "Can I get back to you with that? It won't be long, but I want to check some things before I commit."

"Sure. Just reach out."

"Can I text you at this number?" Ghost needed to ask Robyn about the best place to meet. He had what he wanted in mind, he just needed to find out where it was exactly. And decide when they wanted to meet.

"You can."

"Great, I'll be in touch. I've held off calling in reinforcements and I'd like to get this settled without having to bring others in."

"That would be ideal."

They rang off, Ghost promising to be in touch, then he picked up his coffee cup and sipped it as he sat in the living room, thinking about what needed to happen. If things went well, he and Malice would be able to go back to Gillette sooner rather than later.

That thought stopped him cold. What would happen with Robyn when he went back to Gillette? Yeah, he'd asked about the possibility of getting a place other than the bunk house, but he hadn't talked to her about it. What if she decided she didn't want to go to Gillette to be with him? What if she might be willing, but wasn't ready yet? Was he willing to do the long-distance thing until she was?

He set the empty cup aside and sent off a couple text messages asking both Gizmo and Krissi to find what they could on this Cowboy. Then he pocketed his phone, stood, biting back the groan that fought to escape, then picked up his cup and carried it into the kitchen for a refill.

CHAPTER 39

Robyn appreciated Ghost having Malice bring food. She really did, but making him stay behind and help wasn't necessary, and she found it more irritating than helpful. It seemed like every time she reached for something he was there. She clenched her teeth and refrained from saying anything, but couldn't help but marvel at how different having Malice in her kitchen felt from when it was Ghost.

She hadn't even minded when Ghost had stepped in and cooked, but just the idea of Malice doing the same thing set her teeth on edge. *It won't last long,* she reminded herself as she fried the eggs, assembled the sandwiches, and set them on plates.

"Here, can you take this to Ghost?" She handed one plate to Malice and turned to put away a few items before sitting down with her own sandwich and coffee. Ghost's voice stopped her.

"Turn around with that. I'm coming in there to eat."

She turned back around to find Ghost coming down the short hall from the front of the house. Her heart flipped in her chest as she saw the dark bruises on his face, but she was glad to see him moving easier after how he'd almost curled into a ball this morning from pain. She hurried to put things away so she could sit with him while they ate.

"Did you reach anyone?" Malice asked once they'd all had a few bites.

"I did. I have a meet with some guy called Cowboy later today."

"Where?" Malice asked.

Robyn let her gaze bounce from one to another as they talked as if she wasn't in the room.

"I haven't decided yet. That's part of why I came back here. Sunshine, I need to know a place. Where do all the cops gather for coffee, dinner, that kind of thing? And can we ask your dad if he knows anyone by the name of Cowboy?"

"Sure, there's a diner not far off the 94 where Dad used to go. He still meets some of his friends for coffee, I'll text and see if that's where they still go. And I'll ask about that Cowboy while I'm at it." She didn't miss the wide-eyed look of surprise that Malice shot him. She didn't know if it was because he'd asked her where to go or to ask her father about Cowboy. She didn't really care. What mattered to her was that Ghost had asked.

"Thanks. Once you're sure on the place I'll set the meet," Ghost said. He turned to look at Malice. "I'll want you to arrive early, get a seat and scope the place out. Be there just in case." He turned back to her. "I need you to stay here for this. Okay?"

Robyn nodded. She didn't need to be a part of everything, and if this guy was one of the same group that did that to his face, she didn't want him worrying about her when he should be worrying about staying safe. She hadn't expected to go along anyway. That didn't mean she wouldn't worry while he was gone though.

She finished eating, fetched her phone from the bedroom and sent the message to Dad, then shoved the phone in her sweatpants pocket and turned to survey the kitchen. It wasn't a big mess and she'd rather tackle it now than let it get worse. She started loading the dishwasher and putting away the last of the things she hadn't gotten to earlier, while the men discussed the meet later.

She was lost in her own thoughts when the phone in her pocket vibrated, startling her.

"You okay, sunshine?" Ghost's voice carried concern.

She picked up a towel and dried her hands. "I'm fine. My phone startled me." She pulled out the device and found that Dad had texted her back. She gave Ghost the name of the diner, then read him what Dad had said about the guy he was going to meet.

"I've only ever encountered one man who went by Cowboy that I know of. He was with a rough crowd, but at the time he was only guilty by association. I would warn you to be careful. He hangs with a rough crowd, but I've not heard anything worse of him." She typed up a quick thanks to Dad and hit send, then put her phone away before looking back to Ghost. "Does that help?"

"It does, thanks. If things haven't changed it may mean he's truly looking to apologize and that's all." He pulled out his own phone and sent a couple messages. "I'm setting the meet with this guy at three. That will give us some time to hear back from our contacts. They may have more information. The more we know, the better prepared we'll be."

"Good. You two do what you need to. I'm going to go make the bed." She left the two to do whatever they felt the need to do while she did her best to keep herself busy, at least for a while.

CHAPTER 40

Ghost was aware Robyn was giving him and Malice time to figure out what they were doing. He appreciated that he didn't have to come up with an excuse to send her to the other room. They finished making plans for the meeting with this Cowboy guy, who'd messaged back that he would see Ghost at three as requested, then Ghost sent Malice off to recon the diner and run a few other errands.

With Malice gone, he went looking for Robyn. He didn't have to look far. He found her in the primary bathroom, combing her hair and seeming to get ready for the day.

"Hey, sunshine. What's your plan for today?" He stepped up behind her and set his hands on her hips.

"Not much. I've got a few errands to run, so I thought I would leave about the same time you do. Don't worry." She held up one hand to stop his protest before he could start speaking. "I'm not going anywhere near the diner. I need to hit the bank, the post office, and the grocery store. Last time I went shopping I only got the essentials and even then, I wasn't planning on feeding more than me. I need to get a few more things, even if the two of you wrap up what you've got going on here and head out in the next day or so." She turned and kissed his jaw gently before turning back to the mirror and what she was doing.

He watched her reflection for several seconds, trying to put his thoughts into words, before speaking. "I don't like the idea of you out there unprotected. Not while we're at this meeting or at any other time— no, let me finish," he said when she opened her mouth. She was going to argue, he could tell by the stubborn expression on her face. "I know this is fast, and you're right. My job here may be done sooner rather than later. I like the idea of leaving you here even less. I don't want this to end." He met her gaze in the reflection. "I know this is fast, but I'm working on getting a place of my own in or near Gillette. I'd like you to consider coming back to Wyoming with me."

Her mouth fell open, and she stood staring at him in the mirror, but she didn't say anything. He waited, and still, nothing.

"I'm not asking for a decision now. I'm not even asking you to make a decision yet. Just to consider it. Will you do that, please?"

She stared at him a moment longer then laid down the brush in her hand and spun to face him.

"I can't tell you what I'll decide. I can't even say it will be an easy decision, but I will think about it. Okay?"

"Thinking about it is all I'm asking, at least for today." His gaze flicked from her eyes to her full lips. They were so tempting.

Slowly, taking care of his ribs, he lowered his mouth to cover hers. It started as a sweet kiss, where he couldn't resist tasting her, but it grew. Her hands slid up under his shirt and along his skin at the waist. She tugged him closer until all that separated them was the two layers of their clothing and even those thin barriers were too much. Ghost let his hands slide down her shoulders and along her body.

Robyn's groan and the way she arched into him stirred something deep inside him. Her hands slipped below his waistband and grabbed handfuls of his ass, pulling him against her.

Ghost couldn't hold back the growl that filled him. He let his own hands drift to her waistband. A couple tugs and her pants fell to her feet. He let his hands drift over her, one trailing down to the cleft between her thighs. He used one finger to tease her clit while he trailed his lips from hers, along her jaw, down her neck and along her collar bone as he made his way to suckle on her nipple.

"Jesus, sunshine. You're soaked." He captured her nipple with his mouth and teased the tip with his tongue.

Robyn let out a whimper. Her hips rolled as if seeking his hand. Her fingers dug into his back as she pulled at him, trying to pull him closer.

"God," he muttered after releasing her breast from his mouth. "I was just going to kiss you, but damn. I need you. Now."

He scooped her up under the ass and set her on the edge of the counter, ignoring the throb in his ribs as he stepped between her thighs. Before he could reach for the button of his jeans, her hands were there. She opened his pants and slid her hand inside to cup and squeeze his erection. He groaned.

"Don't tease me, sunshine. I need you."

She looked up and met his gaze through her lashes as one hand flat against his stomach pushed him a step back.

Was she telling him no?

Then she dipped her head and covered the tip of his cock with her mouth. The hot moisture and delicious swirl of her tongue against his sensitive head nearly had him exploding right then and there.

Without thinking about it, he buried his hand in her hair.

"Oh god, sunshine. That feels so good. But you've got to stop." He tugged at her hair, trying not to hurt her, but to pull her off his cock. As much as he hated to admit it, if she didn't stop soon, he was going to lose control, and in her mouth was not where he wanted to come, not this time.

She pulled back and looked up at him through her lashes again. "What do you want?"

"You, right here. Just lean back."

"I don't have any condoms in here."

He pulled one from his pocket. He'd tucked a couple there when he'd gotten dressed; just in case he'd found a chance today. It wasn't what he'd had in mind when he'd come in here, but he'd been hopeful when he'd sent Malice away.

"Ohh. I like a man who's prepared." She snagged it from his fingers, ripped it open and unrolled it over him before lifting her sweatshirt off over her head, tossing it aside and leaning back, bracing her hands on the counter as she spread her legs wider. "You were going to show me something?" She grinned up at him, as if she had an idea what he was thinking.

Ghost reached for her and between her touch and taste, quickly lost track of time as he lost himself in her.

*

Ghost walked into the diner where he was meeting Cowboy, stopped, and looked around. There were about twenty-five tables scattered throughout the room, with about a half dozen of them taken. Fewer people in the place was part of why he'd set the meet here, but if this guy knew much about the area, he'd know this was where the police hung out. And if Ghost was lucky, one or two would stop in while he was here talking to the guy.

"Seat yourself, I'll be right with you," an older woman in an apron said as she passed by with a plate in each hand.

Another quick scan let him know where Malice sat, he headed in that direction and chose a table that was still several seats away. Enough that he wouldn't easily overhear what was being said but if Ghost needed help, he'd be close by and could be there in next to no time.

Ghost sat and looked around. The wood paneling and laminate tabletops spoke of an older place, but given the rest of the town, he wasn't surprised. Especially with what he knew about cops, they had a tendency to find places they liked, and keep going there, especially if the coffee was good.

A minute or two after he arrived, the waitress appeared with a glass of water and a menu.

"I'm meeting someone here, but I'll have a cup of coffee in the meantime," he said.

"Coming right up," she left him with the menu and hurried off. Ghost scanned the menu while he waited. He might have something small, but he planned to wait and eat with Robyn later.

The waitress had come with his coffee then left him to look over the menu when the bell over the door rang, making Ghost look up. A man wearing a leather jacket stepped inside, looked around and headed his way as if he knew exactly where he was going. He stopped beside Ghost's table.

"My name's Cowboy. I don't think I ever asked for yours."

Ghost motioned to the seat on the other side of the table. "I'm Ghost. Have a seat and talk to me. You said you had news?"

"I do." The newcomer pulled out the chair opposite Ghost and sat. When the waitress came by with a glass of water and a menu, he waived her off and said, "Just coffee please. I don't know how long I'll be here."

She nodded and hurried off.

"First off, I want to apologize for what happened to you. Tank and a few others were running some operations behind the rest of my club's back. We found out about them after the raid that rescued you." He shook his head. "We really should have figured it out. The signs were there, we just weren't looking for them."

Ghost watched him in silence for several moments, trying to read his face and judge his sincerity. He didn't seem to be lying, that didn't mean he wasn't.

"Tell me why I should believe you. Start with how you knew exactly who you were coming to see?"

"There was video surveillance at Tank's. That's how they knew you were there watching them. I saw it this morning and watched Rooster roust you out of your truck and walk you into the house."

Fear shot through Ghost. If they had that on video, they also had a video of Robyn getting into his truck and driving away. If they could identify him, they could identify her. She could be in danger because he'd let her pick up his truck. He mentally called himself ten kinds of stupid for letting her pick up his truck.

"We're not looking for the girl, if that's your concern." Cowboy's voice was calm, and Ghost mentally kicked himself again for being so transparent. What happened to his ability to keep a blank face? He knew the answer as soon as he asked himself the question. Robyn had happened. The waitress returned with Cowboy's coffee, asked if they wanted anything else and left.

"Tell me why we're here." Ghost wanted to get down to the facts. They weren't here just for an apology.

Cowboy watched him a moment then took a deep breath and spoke.

"After the raid, we started looking into Tank. Not only did we find what he did to you, we also found his ties to a group down south, and that they had him, and by extension, the Kings, harassing you and your friends in Gillette. That is over as of today."

"What part is over?"

"All of it. After the raid, we saw the video and investigated, then we turned Tank, Rooster, and a couple others over to the police, along with the video. We want nothing to do with someone that stupid. They've been stripped of their positions and their patches. What they've done is not who the Kings are." He looked down at the table, paused while the waitress came by and refilled their cups, then once she was gone, continued. "Don't get me wrong, we're no angels, but stalking, kidnapping, assault?" He shook his head. "We try to stay under the radar and Tank threw that rule out the window and was throwing all of us under the bus for his own gain."

"You said he was working with some group down south. Tell me more about them."

Cowboy shrugged. "He did time with some bigwig a while back. Not the head of the club, but someone with pull. They had him put men on your ranch in Wyoming, harass the women coming and going. It probably would have gone farther but they traded places with another pair, and you followed them home."

Ghost bit back a growl. They hadn't told him that someone had taken the place of these two asshats in Gillette. Probably because he would want to come back and take care of them. He pushed that out of his mind. "Do you know the group name?"

Cowboy nodded and looked grim. "I do. It took some digging to find, and I don't remember the exact name as it's in Spanish, but it translates to the crazy devils."

"Son of a bitch. I was afraid of that." Ghost didn't bother to keep the anger out of his tone. He hated that he was revealing that much to the stranger but couldn't seem to help himself.

"I take it you know who they are?"

"I do and the Spanish you don't recall is Los Diablos Locos. We have ongoing issues with them."

"That's the one. They after you guys for a reason?"

"Too many to go into right now. I thought we had come to a truce, if not a peace, but apparently, I was wrong. My president isn't going to be happy."

"I don't want to get in the middle of that. We've ousted the troublemakers in the Kings and these Diablos are hopefully too far away to get too upset that we've cut ties. But you aren't so far away. I questioned everyone involved. They say you're a club, they are sure of it, but no one can tell me who you are."

Ghost couldn't resist a smirk. They'd deliberately not worn kuttes in Wyoming, not yet. They were trying to build goodwill for the ranch first, then they'd let the locals know who the club was. They weren't keeping that they were a club secret, just building some goodwill before they were obvious about it. "We're the Demented Souls. Our issues with the Diablos aren't new and don't stem from where we are in Wyoming. They come from our original charter in Arizona, much closer to his in New Mexico. You shouldn't have to worry about them coming up here after you."

"I'm glad to hear it's not that they're venturing north."

"I'm not saying that's not possible, but it's not why they're after us. In all likelihood, they only reached out this far because we had something that took us north."

"Good. Now that that's settled, we still owe you. What Tank and his men did to you should never have happened." Cowboy motioned to Ghost's face and down his body. "He had no intention of letting you go. Even though the Kings have no beef with you. We don't hold with that. Which is why he's out and disavowed. The rest of us want to make this right between the Kings and the Souls."

Ghost watched him a moment, trying to decide what to say next.

"I don't want to say I speak for the Souls. I don't. I only speak for me. But personally, I want to know what authority you have to speak from." Ghost gave the right breast of Cowboy's kutte, which he wore under the heavier leather jacket a pointed look. There was no patch there telling Ghost his position in the club.

Cowboy lifted one hand then balled it into a fist as if stopping himself from touching the area. "I ripped the old one off this morning. The one that said VP, but I haven't had a chance to put the President patch on yet." Cowboy shook his head, then met Ghost's gaze again. "I have been cleaning up messes and putting out fires all day, and I suspect I'm nowhere near done. I led the revolt to oust Tank and his followers. Everyone who knew what was going on, or why he was doing it, is gone, or will be as soon as we find them. This is personal to me, and I want to be sure you and the Souls don't hold it against us."

Ghost watched him for a moment, he couldn't accept the offer. Not without checking with leadership, and after what had happened, did he trust this guy?

"Let me take your offer to my club. I can give recommendations, and I can tell them that before today I never saw you. I can't guarantee what the decision will be."

"I can accept that. Take my case to them. Tell them that we feel like we've done the Demented Souls wrong, and we want to make it right. You have my number. You can reach out day or night and if I don't respond right away, I'll get back to you when I have an answer."

"Sounds good. Is that all you're going to have?" Cowboy nodded to Ghost's coffee.

"That was my plan."

"I'll get it. I'm the whole reason you are here anyway." He stood and went to the counter.

Ghost watched as he paid the ticket and left. He was still finishing his coffee when Malice came from behind him and took the seat Cowboy had been in.

"I couldn't hear more than one word in five. What did he have to say?"

Ghost didn't have to look around to know no one else was close enough to hear, so he filled in Malice on what had been said, at least as much as he could without giving up too much information on the Souls. He didn't go into why the Souls had issues with the Diablos, Malice would learn those details soon enough, if he decided to patch in.

When they'd finished discussing the meet with Cowboy, Ghost asked Malice to keep an eye on the clubhouse. He wanted to know if any of the faces they knew, the men who had been in on Ghost's capture, including Tank, and the ones they'd followed up here, were around. When he was done giving instructions, they parted ways. Malice went off to either watch the clubhouse or back to the motel, Ghost went back to Robyn's house.

CHAPTER 41

After Ghost and Malice left, Robyn looked around the house, noting how natural it seemed to have Ghost here. He filled corners she hadn't realized were empty, at least it seemed that way. She wished she could have gone with him, but understood why he hadn't wanted her along. If this group that had hurt him knew who she was, it might put her in danger.

With a sigh and a shake of her head at the direction of her thoughts, she pulled on her coat and grabbed her keys. If she was going to be feeding three instead of one, she needed more food in the house.

At the grocery store she was working her way up and down the aisles, stocking up on what she thought she would need for at least a couple more days of having the guys around.

"You're looking better," a familiar voice said from nearby.

Robyn looked up to find Bobby standing a few feet away.

"Thank you. Oddly, I feel so much better when I'm not accosted by some stranger demanding to know where a mystery person is. Did you ever find out what was going on with that?" She hadn't meant to ask, but curiosity got the better of her.

"No, and I don't expect to. Officers Carlton and Dockter took him with them, I don't know if they took him to jail or for some kind of treatment, but I haven't seen him since. The officers have been in but they're busy and probably wouldn't tell me if I asked," he said with a shrug. He motioned to her cart. "Looks like you're stocking up for a storm. Is there one moving in?"

"Not that I know of. I've got some guests in from out of town." She smiled and hoped he wouldn't push for more. She didn't like telling too many people that Ghost was staying with her. Not that she had any reason to hide it, but he'd already been attacked once, she wanted him to be safe at her place.

"Oh, nice! Enjoy your company, have a good day." He moved on down the aisle, probably going back to whatever, he'd been doing when he spotted her.

Robyn finished her shopping and took her cart out to her car. She was in the middle of loading her purchases into the truck when someone stepped up behind her and started helping her move bags from the cart to her trunk, she twisted around and found Dad.

"Good afternoon, sweetheart." He leaned in and gave her a hug. "I hear they found your missing friend. He was in rough shape but nothing serious, right?"

"Yeah, he's sore and a little cranky but he'll be okay. Thanks so much for your help, Dad." She didn't know if calling him had helped get people moving to find Ghost, but she was sure it hadn't hurt.

Dad leaned back and looked her up and down, focusing on her face since the rest of her was bundled up against the cold.

"You look happy. Happier than I've seen you in a long time." He tilted his head and narrowed his eyes. "Is it this guy you were looking for?"

Robyn couldn't help the smile that spread across her face. She realized she found herself smiling a lot more since meeting Ghost.

"Yeah, I think it is. I like him, Dad, really like him. He feels right. And best of all, he makes me feel safe and like I'm finally home." She shook her head, knowing she sounded silly. "I know I haven't known him long, but I think I love him."

"As long as he treats you right, he'll have my vote. I love you, sweetheart. Get in out of this cold. I'm going to get a few things, but we'll be in touch. I want to hear more about this guy of yours."

"Will do." She couldn't help the laugh that escaped. Would Dad like Ghost? "Take care and I love you." She hugged Dad again then he went inside, taking her cart with him, and she got into the car. Would Ghost be back yet? She hoped so.

On the drive home she wondered how things had gone with the guy from the other club. Would the meeting mean Ghost's business in Dickenson was through? Would it be time for him to go back to Wyoming? The idea weighed heavily on her, not just on her mind, but she felt it like a stone in her stomach. What would she do if he told her he was leaving?

She didn't want to think about it, but she hated hiding from the truth and she knew he would have to go back eventually. There was nothing stopping him from having to go back now if they wrapped up what brought him here to begin with. She'd known it was coming all along and had just ignored it and hoped it wouldn't be a big deal when the time came.

Robyn pushed the what if thoughts out of her head as she pulled into the driveway. Ghost's truck wasn't back yet but that was probably a good thing because she hadn't thought to give him a key.

⁂

She'd just finished carrying everything in and gone back out to lock up her car when Ghost pulled up in Malice's truck. She closed up her car and hit the lock button while he got out and came around the front of the truck.

"How did everything go?" she couldn't keep herself from asking.

"Better than I'd hoped." He followed her inside. "Did you just get home?"

"Yep, just got everything carried in. Now I have to deal with it all." She headed for the kitchen to get at least the cold stuff put away. He followed and as she started pulling things out of bags and sorting, he helped. When she went to the fridge, he handed her what went inside.

"Are you going to go back to Wyoming soon?" she asked as she closed the refrigerator and opened the freezer to put those items away.

"Soon, probably, in a few days."

She tried not to let the news crush her. They still had a few days together. She would make the most of them.

CHAPTER 42

Something was off with Robyn. He got back to the house shortly after she did. She'd already carried everything in, but he pitched in and helped her put the food away. He couldn't help but notice there was a lot, or it seemed like it to him.

He got his first clue when she asked if he had to go back to Wyoming soon. Was she worried about him leaving? Was she already mentally breaking up with him? Not if he had anything to say about it.

"How about we go out and do some thing fun tonight?" he suggested as they gathered up the reusable bags she'd used for the groceries and put them away.

Robyn closed the cabinet door and watched him for a moment.

"We can go out if you want."

"But?" He watched her back, there was something in her tone that told him she didn't want to go out.

"But nothing." She shrugged. "I'll go get ready to go out. What do you want to do?" Robyn headed for the bedroom, he followed, something was off, and he intended to figure out what.

She went into the bedroom and stopped in front of the closet, scanning what was on the rack. He stepped up behind her and wrapped his arms around her waist.

"We don't have to go out if you don't want to. It was just a suggestion. I'd be just as happy to stay here and spend the evening just the two of us."

Some of the tension drained from her body.

"Would you really?" She sounded uncertain.

"I would. It's about spending time with you, not what we're doing."

She spun in his arms, tilted her head back and looked up at him. "You'd really be okay with spending the evening here at the house?"

"Not only would I not mind, I will enjoy it just as much if not more. Because I'll be here with you, and you'll be happier here. Do you have something in mind for our evening? Or just that we not go out?"

"I had a few things in mind, starting with dinner. What exactly we do other than that depends on if it's just us or if Malice will be here too."

"He may be spending some time here over the next few days, but he'll be doing other things too. Tonight he's got something to do and won't be coming by."

"I can work with that." She stretched up and brushed her lips against his.

Ghost couldn't resist the temptation. He tightened his arms around her middle, teased her lips open and kissed her for all he was worth. Her hands came up to grip his arms and she melted into him. He loved the way she felt in his arms. The last thing he wanted to do was walk away from her.

What would it take to convince her to go back to Wyoming with him?

She pulled away, breaking the kiss as she dropped back onto her heels.

"I don't want to hurt you."

"You'd have a hard time hurting me, sunshine."

"Even your ribs?" She laid a hand over where the worst of the bruising there was.

"That might hurt a little, but it's only temporary. Tell me more about these plans of yours." He tried to steer the subject to something more pleasant.

"Well, I got enough to feed us all for a few days. I though I'd cook us dinner, then we could find something to watch or maybe play a game."

"What kind of game you have in mind?"

"I only have a couple games, and several decks of cards." Her grin turned coy. "I do have a package of index cards. We can write sexual favors and use those to bet. Basically, dirty poker."

Ghost kissed the tip of her nose.

"I like the way you think." He released her to see what she wanted to do first.

"Your meet at the diner, did you eat anything while you were there?"

"No. I just had coffee. I planned to have dinner with you."

"You're sweet." She stretched up and kissed his jaw.

"Never, ever say that to anyone but me. I have a reputation to uphold and sweet is not part of it."

She turned and headed for the kitchen, just before she disappeared from sight she turned and glanced at him over her shoulder.

"What's that secret worth to you?"

Ghost couldn't keep the grin from his face as he followed her. What was it about this woman?

🐟

Later, after they'd finished dinner, they sat on the sofa, both turned sideways, facing each other. Robyn pulled out a deck of cards and rather than mess with writing sexual favors on cards, Ghost suggested they play a few hands to warm up, then they could play for kisses.

She narrowed her eyes at him, as if she could tell he was up to something and was trying to figure out what.

"No tricks." He held his hands up in front of him as if he were surrendering. "Besides, either way we play, it's really a no loss for both of us."

"I'm not so sure about that." She continued to watch him with narrowed eyes, but Ghost could tell her skepticism was an act.

She dealt the first hand. Ghost paid more attention to her than to his own hand and she won it easily. The next two hands went much the same way as he watched her, looking for tells, more than he bothered to pay attention to his own hand.

After a few hands, she handed him the deck.

"Your turn to deal. Maybe you'll pay more attention to what we're doing then. Not that I'm complaining. I could stand to win a bunch of kisses from you."

"No problem." Ghost took the cards and began dealing. "What would it take for you to consider coming back to Wyoming with me?"

She looked up from her cards, eyes wide.

"D— do you mean that? You mentioned it before, but I thought it was heat of the moment. I didn't know you were serious."

"I do. I wouldn't screw with you like that."

Robyn stared at him for ten seconds, then blinked rapidly several times.

"You don't have to answer right away, but think about it. I talked to my foreman on my way back this afternoon. He said there's a cabin on the ranch I can have. It's older and needs some work, but everything's functional, if not exactly pretty." He didn't tell her some of the other things they'd talked about. Like Cowboy's background check and club business.

"Cabin?"

He couldn't tell if she was still trying to absorb the idea or if the idea of a cabin was a deal breaker for her. "Well, that's what I call it. It's one of the smaller places on the ranch and the outer walls look like cut logs. If I remember right, it was once the cook slash housekeeper's house."

She frowned. "How big is this ranch?"

"I've heard different numbers, but between what Tuck owns and the leased land? Around a hundred thousand acres."

She stared until he reached over and closed her mouth for her. Then she looked down at the cards between them but didn't seem to register what to do with them.

"You really want me to go to Wyoming with you? Like to live?" Her gaze flicked back up to watch him.

"Yes, to live. Why else would I need a house? We also don't have to do this all at once. I can go back, move into the house and we can visit back and forth. Though I hate thinking of that much space, not to mention time, between us."

She still watched him, not saying anything.

Great. She thought he was crazy for moving so fast. He didn't know how to back this down, and he didn't want to. He wanted to be with her. All the time. He dropped his gaze to the cards in his hands, shook his head and let out a wry chuckle.

"I never thought I'd be the one moving faster than the other person wanted." He was still staring at his hands, wondering what would happen now, when her hand covered his. He looked up to find her watching him.

"It's not that you're moving faster than I want. You just surprised me. I wasn't prepared. I want to be with you. I hate the idea of a long-distance relationship. We can make it work short term, if we need to, but longer than a few weeks," Robyn shook her head, "I think it would be extremely difficult."

"Really?" Hope surged through him, though it wasn't lost on him that now he was the one not believing what he was hearing.

"Really. But there's a lot to consider. If I move in with you, that's housing taken care of, but what would I do? How would I cover my share of the bills, and before you say it, I'm not going to let you support me. I need to be making my own way. Even if I have a job, how am I going to get all my things down there that I need to take? What will I do with this place? It's mine. My grandmother left it to me."

"I'm sure we can find you a job. If not something on the ranch, then Gillette is about twenty minutes away. It's about the size of Dickenson. There are a lot of jobs. As for moving you? We've got two pickups right here. We can load them up and haul whatever we need. If we need more room, we can rent a trailer. If you'll come with me this trip, I'll get a dolly and we'll tow your car. Then we can fill it with stuff too, if you want. As for this place?" He looked around. "Keep it. Rent it out. That will give you some income without working." He held up one hand to stop the protest she'd already started to make. "I'm not saying don't work. I'm saying it will give you time to find something."

"You've put some thought into this." She sounded amazed.

Ghost didn't know if he should be thankful or surprised.

"I have about some things; others just are what they are. We can deal with anything we want to deal with. It's all about how bad you want it."

She picked up the cards on the sofa between them, then took the rest of the deck from his hands and set it on the table sitting in front of the couch. She went up on her hands and knees and closed the distance between the two of them.

"I want it. I want all of it. I want you." She moved up his body until she could kiss him.

Ghost wrapped his arms around her and tugged, trying to get her to sit in his lap.

"I don't want to hurt you."

"I'll let you know if you hurt me. Come sit down and let's figure things out." He tugged her down into his lap, this time she went without fighting him. "Now, details. What do you want to take to Wyoming with us?"

She was quiet a moment. "That depends."

"On what?"

"How much furniture is in this cabin; do you know off hand?"

"Not at all, I'm not sure I've ever been inside." He picked up his phone and pulled up the texting app, then sent a message to Lurch asking what kind of furniture is in the house and what might need to be replaced. "What else?"

"We need to figure out how long you need to stay in town or if you'll need to come back. I assume the guy who did this to you is in custody and going to be prosecuted?"

"I've heard they caught him. He wasn't in the house when they found me."

"It's my turn to reach out. What was his name again?" She picked up her phone from where it had been sitting on the couch between them earlier and texted her dad, asking about Tank and the others after he told her the names he knew.

"Okay, next question?"

"How long do we have to get ready? There is a lot I will need to do. I need to let Dad know, give notice at work, pack up everything. How long can you stay while I get ready?"

He was glad to hear excitement in her voice, even if there was a bit of anxiety there as well. Not that he blamed her for the anxiety, it was a big decision and a lot of work. And they didn't have a lot of time to stretch it out. Or at least he didn't want to take that kind of time, and it seemed she didn't either.

"If we can make it happen in the next couple weeks, I can work it out. We might need to send Malice back before then, so we'll need to figure out what we can send with him."

"You'll also need to get your truck back from him before he goes."

Ghost bit his lip and scrubbed the back of his neck with one hand.

"Actually, the truck Malice has is a ranch truck. We came up in that one. I bought this one while we were here. We needed a vehicle the guys who had been watching the ranch wouldn't recognize while we watched them to figure out who they were."

She turned and stared at him a moment.

"You bought a truck because you needed something that wouldn't be recognized. Did it not occur to you to rent one?"

Ghost shrugged. "I needed a truck of my own up here anyway. We came up from Arizona in a moving truck and on our bikes, though we're not riding the bikes much now."

Robyn blinked several times then turned back around.

"So, we don't need to worry about switching vehicles. But if he's going back before us, we either need to get the trailer and pack it before he goes back or send him back with my car, which also means packing it before he leaves. Either way it means I need to get boxes."

They discussed what they needed to do and put together a to do list until Ghost's phone rang almost an hour later.

"It's Malice," he said before hitting the button to answer it.

"What have you learned?"

"No sign of Tank an several others at their clubhouse."

"That's good, but they could be laying low, so we believe Cowboy's story." In his lap, Robyn picked up her phone, read a text that had come in and replied.

"I thought of that. There's also no sign anyone has been to Tank's house. The crime scene tape is still across the door."

"Again, good, but not definitive. I could get in and out of that house without you knowing, even if you watched it twenty-four seven. Any activity from the asshats we tailed up here?"

"The truck is sitting at the clubhouse. Hasn't moved in thirty-six hours."

"You set eyes on it or trusting the blip on the screen?"

"I've checked it a couple times. So far, the truck hasn't moved, either on the screen or from parking space."

"Good job. It's good to know but not definitive. I've got some other feelers out that should let us know more. Why don't you call it a night?

Get some sleep and we'll figure out where to go from here in the morning."

Malice's sigh echoed across the line. "Coffee and breakfast again tomorrow?"

"Let me check." Ghost pulled the phone from his ear, covered the mic with his thumb and spoke to Robyn. "You want him to bring anything in the morning?"

"Just whatever he wants in his coffee besides sugar," she said, then went back to texting.

He put the phone back to his ear. "No, just show up and not too early or you'll be waiting in the truck."

"What's too early?"

Ghost relayed the question to Robyn.

"Seven," she said, never looking up from her phone where her thumbs seemed to dance across the screen.

"Eight," he told Malice.

"You do know I heard her, right?"

"Know, don't care. I plan to sleep in and don't want her getting up for you instead of resting with me." He finished the call with Malice and disconnected then turned his attention back to Robyn, who still sat in his lap, texting. "Good conversation?"

"Informative." She typed up a message and hit send, then looked up at him. "You'll want to hear this." She scrolled up several messages and reviewed them while she summarized.

"Dad says they arrested several men yesterday afternoon, one was Tank. He doesn't have names on the others. Judge set no bail at the arraignment this afternoon. He says from his experience you shouldn't have to testify. Where you were found along with your medical records, you will have to sign a release on those, should be enough for conviction."

"That's great. Did you let him know you're coming to Wyoming with me?"

Robyn shook her head. "That's a conversation that needs to be in person. I set up lunch with him tomorrow. I'd like you to come."

Ghost frowned. Was she afraid to tell her dad she was moving? Did she want him there to back her up?

"I want you to meet him. I think he'll like you. And I know he'll feel better about all this if he's met you and you're not just some nebulous stranger he's never even seen."

Relief washed through him. "I can do that." He tugged her close. "You're sure you want to do this? You're ready to leave all this behind and come to Wyoming with me?"

"I can't think of anything I'd rather do. I'm excited." She looked up at him, then stretched up to kiss his jaw. "You know I love you, right?"

"It's a good thing because I think I fell a while ago. I don't know what I'd do if you didn't want to come with me." He chuckled. "I take that back. I know exactly what I'd do. I'd spend every spare moment I could here with you, and the rest of the time in darkness. I know it sounds corny, but you are my sunshine, Robyn. You make my world bright, no matter what else is going on."

Thank you for reading Demented Souls book #12, Ghost. If you enjoyed it, or even if you didn't, please consider leaving an honest review at your favorite retailer or two.

If you're looking for more from Melissa Stevens please consider joining her VIP reader list for weekly updates on what she's working on now, as well as specials, giveaways and more.

All of her works can be found on her website at http://melissastevens.us